THE
DE-EVOLUTION
BUG

THE
DE-EVOLUTION
BUG

VAIBHAV MUKIM

Srishti
Publishers & Distributors

SRISHTI PUBLISHERS & DISTRIBUTORS
Registered Office: N-16, C.R. Park
New Delhi – 110 019

Corporate Office: 212A, Peacock Lane
Shahpur Jat, New Delhi – 110 049
editorial@srishtipublishers.com

First published by
Srishti Publishers & Distributors in 2017

What is life which does not struggle. A worm which does not fight. A fly which will not flap its wings when caught in a spider's web.

What is life which does not find beauty in the mundane, knowing it will end one day.

This book is dedicated to the struggle within. May we all win one day.

Acknowledgements

We are Vaibhav. We are not one. We never wanted to be one. So we became many. We are his neurons. We do the heavy lifting, or so we would like to believe.

This book was difficult to write because we kept bickering with each other. But certain other neurons helped us through it all.

We would like to thank Stuti's neurons. Though it is a bit of a cliché to thank your own editor, we have come to the consensus that this book, whatever shape and form you find it in, is largely because of her.

Then we would like to show our gratitude to all the neurons we met along the way which fired us in directions we didn't even know existed.

Some of Anujit Roy's neurons helped us a great deal. So did Devashish Goel's. Not to forget Aditya Tripathi and his unique set of neurons.

Then there were Sharad Das Gupta's extremely enlightened neurons. Last but not least, there were Esha Rajput's neurons which insisted we write this book in the first place.

And then there are your neurons. The ones we intend to tickle and thrill. Thank you for reading.

The package lay on the terrace. It was dropped by an airplane a few hours ago. This was one of the many packets to have made it to the sixty feet by thirty feet roof of their house. The package was also the solitary reminder of the family's predicament.

The town was infested by zombies. Thousands of them roamed the streets. They rattled doors and windows. They pushed and howled. Their terrifying howls were the only sound that broke the dreaded silence of the dark and undead night. The sudden appearance of the moon from behind the clouds painted a strange picture of the night, a ghastly one.

The house was surrounded by more than two hundred bodies, roving relentlessly. They moved from one spot to another, trying to find a weak spot to force their way in.

They could obviously smell the four human beings inside. The virus, which could single-handedly wipe out the entire horde, would be released in the air at 6 a.m.

This virus was capable of detaching the brain from the spinal cord within a matter of hours. Death was expected to follow instantaneously. But, there was a catch. The virus was ruthless and could not discriminate between zombies and humans.

The Swiss government had invented the killer virus about two years ago. It was the answer to a terrorist threat that had grown in the Eastern side of the world. But now it would be used for a different kind of threat. One that didn't care for religion or race. Its one and only aim was multiplication.

The timing of the virus' release was critical because people on the ground were quickly running out of options. Packages containing the antidote to the virus were dropped by airplanes every twelve hours. This was humanity's only hope against the gruesome deaths which would engulf the city once the killer virus was let loose.

While there was hope, the streets outside were ruled by blood-thirsty zombies who wanted to wipe out all of human inhabitation. Their spiralling hunger to transform every living human into a zombie, into one of their kind, seemed insatiable. Thousands were infected each day. The day was not far when the entire population would kneel in front of these death phantoms and succumb to despair. Amid this widespread animosity, humans still deserved a chance to survive and foster the generations to come.

Apart from the moon, there was no visible source of light in the city of Stillwater, Oklahoma.

Inside Sebastian's house, the moonlight streamed in patches. All four members of the family sat close to each other. It was 10:01 p.m. by Sebastian's watch. They barely had eight hours to go before the virus was released and killed everything in its path. Eight hours to retrieve the package, collect the antidote to the virus and inoculate themselves before the massacre began.

He was sitting in the drawing room with his family while they brainstormed to find ways to get the package safely indoors.

In the moonlight that streamed through the first-floor windows, he could see Pat, his sister.

Pat was thirty-five and two years older to Sebastian. She was pursuing her Ph.D. in Economics from the London School of Economics and was here for her study break. Sebastian remembered how bossy she had been while they grew up together, a veritable know-it-all.

Most decisions in Sebastian's early life – like what he would do after school, which college he would go to, what he would do after college, which company he would join, where he would live – were dominated by Pat.

Now as Sebastian watched her, he could see that Pat's domineering nature had been a shell. She was behaving strangely.

Pat's brain had ceased to function, or so it seemed. She was chewing on one fingernail, then another, then on a bunch of her hair, then back to her fingernails. Pat's manner was hypnotic, repetitive, like she was under a spell. All this while she made a low moaning sound, as if inhaling air caused her great misery.

Sebastian was sitting on the foot of a flight of stairs that led up to the terrace.

To his right, on two gigantic couches, sat his parents, Quentin and Laura. They were a middle-aged couple who had been together for thirty-six years.

Quentin was rubbing his long beard but said nothing.

He ran a successful business with three big factories which manufactured drilling equipment. Quentin has always been the man in charge, someone who always had a plan.

Tonight, he struggled with a stony silence. He wasn't as numb as Pat or Laura, though. His brain had not given up yet. It was still in control and guided his reflexes, or so it seemed. Perhaps decades of running a successful business compelled him to think that he could get out of any situation, however grave or unviable it may be.

Sebastian's mother Laura, who was sitting next to Quentin, held the armrests tightly between her clenched hands, looking at one person then another, but registered nothing, no one.

Sebastian opened his mouth, not out of inspiration, but because someone had to say something to break this horrific silence. The clock was ticking. Someone had to race against time, and also the walking dead who jeopardised the family's very survival as they tried to enter the house through every possible crevice.

"So one person stands watch for the zombie, and the other goes out onto the terrace and retrieves the package," he said. It was the most obvious solution. Suddenly, he became the centre of everyone's attention. This very interjection by Sebastian gathered muffled but curious response from the rest of the family. Yet, he suspected, no matter how obvious the suggestion was, it was one the family would not have reached had they spent hours brainstorming, given the mental state they were in.

"There could be more than one on the terrace," said Laura. She seemed glad to have something to talk about, to focus on, something to combat the rampant dread of death and darkness.

Their largest and only problem, thought Sebastian as he rounded-up his plans and laid out the tasks which were to be undertaken by them as a family, was that a zombie had already made it to the terrace by climbing the sturdy oak tree that stood in the backyard. Now, the zombie sat perched on the roof of the small makeshift gym that Laura had constructed for herself on the terrace.

No one knew how it would react if a human being was introduced to the situation.

If intimidated, it might run off or attack. 'One bite was all it took to become one of them, to turn unhuman,' Sebastian reminded himself. He decided on a course of action which would not alert the zombie, but help retrieve the package.

Quentin cleared his throat, yearning to say something. But as he opened his mouth, he was betrayed by both, voice and words.

'Who else but I,' Sebastian thought, 'can venture out quietly, keep my nerve steady, walk twelve feet across the terrace, which was flooded with moonlight, under the watchful eye of the zombie, collect the package, and then walk quietly back?'

"Well," Quentin tried harder this time and managed to speak, "We haven't heard any noise from the terrace. It is possible that the zombie up there has already left."

"But what if it hasn't?" Laura said. "If you attract its attention now, there will be more of them. And we all know what will happen then." Her words were heavy with contempt and her voice was full of despair.

But Laura was right. Going to the terrace came with a huge risk. One small mistake was enough to attract the entire herd of blood-thirsty monsters. The terrace door would not withstand their might.

Sebastian dropped the decision of going to the terrace and they were back to where they started from.

The brainstorming session hadn't been great. They needed plan B.

The outbreak had started in Oklahoma, USA on 3 August, 2017.

A sewer rat had bitten a little girl at 12:15 p.m. The girl was walking from Westminster St. to Affic Avenue with her parents, when the rat suddenly appeared from the sewer and with a single mindedness of intent that animals display sometimes, had taken a piece out of the little girl's bare ankle.

The girl leapt in alarm. As if on cue, a spasm rippled across her body and to the complete shock and dismay of her parents, she fell on the pavement, dead.

Her mother dropped her shopping bags and kneeled down beside her, massaging her face. Her father checked her pulse and felt none. It was then that he started shouting for help.

After two agonizing minutes, during which they were surrounded by a crowd and an ambulance siren could be heard approaching, the little girl came back to life.

Nobody had any idea about what happened to that little girl in those two minutes because while it's hard to escape a zombie, it's even harder to ask them about the afterlife while you're at it.

But after those two minutes, which ticked away in the mysterious silence of the afterlife, the fate of Stillwater city changed forever.

Down on Hester St., the little girl, who was seven years old when alive, woke up, grabbed her mother's hair, hauled her closer and bit into her neck.

Her mother beat against her daughter's abnormally powerful grip as she tried to break free, but in vain.

And a second later, she too spasmed and fell flat on the floor.

The sympathetic and helpful crowd transformed into a petrified bunch of humans. They stepped backwards, collectively.

The girl's father had no time to react.

The very next minute, the crowd stood witness as the girl got up and jumped at her father. She wrapped her hands around his back and dug her teeth violently into his chest. Her eyes were red with anger and teeth were covered in blood as she craved to expand her territory and go for her next kill.

The crowd was still wondering what to do when the girl turned towards them. For a moment, she seemed puzzled.

And then the crowd made a mistake. It dissipated as people began running in different directions.

This seemed to please the little girl who was randomly chasing, biting and infecting people in the crowd.

By this time, her mother and father woke up as well. It was in a series of such two minutes that the entire population of Stillwater fell prey to the gruesome outbreak. The outbreak which turned the city into a keep full of the undead, mindlessly bent on turning every human being into their own kind.

The city was trapped in terror as the blood-thirsty transformed humans roamed desperate to infect all others, to convert humanity into their own kind, without aid of bibles and priests, to turn the world into zombies. The hapless crowd panicked and stampeded for survival. They started randomly locking themselves inside any establishment they could find. But these predators knew no boundaries. They shattered the windows and forced themselves into the hastily-searched-for hideouts.

The streets were soaked in blood and there was chaos everywhere. One could hear gunshots and sounds of people screaming, running and fighting.

The clamour died out soon after, wrapping the city in an

abominable lull. The only noise left behind was the screeching of the zombies, looking for fresh prey.

Shops had been ransacked, water pipes had burst, gas lines had exploded. In short, the city had transformed into an intimidating territory, a war zone.

A few zombies had been injured, some limped and crawled, while the majority were intact. And they were hunting voraciously.

Hunger did not bother zombies. It was of little concern. When a zombie is hungry, it devours the weakest zombie around as an immediate response. The lame ones were finished first, or the ones with bullet or knife wounds. There was no mercy in their world. Even children were not spared.

These unearthly creatures were on a mission to multiply, to bite and infect the maximum number of human beings and eventually annihilate the entire human race. In pursuit, they behaved like well-oiled machines, like highly capable predators. Zombies were hideous and agile. They could calculate the odds of success and decide when to attack. And it seemed that they were evolving, becoming better at the trade with each kill.

In repose, they possessed fit, well-toned bodies and strong jaws with venomous teeth ready to attack. They were thinking beings, with an inclination to survive.

Except for when a zombie felt a feeding frenzy. Then it would throw itself upon its prey without thinking about its own safety. A fanatical state that threatened and possessed a zombie when it saw a human.

Stillwater, Oklahoma fell to their deluge almost overnight.

Although this relentless biting spree had pushed most of them outwards from the epicentre of the epidemic, a large portion of zombies had stayed back. They broke down doors and windows, infecting those who were hiding and hoping that this nightmare would end. But the zombies spared no one. There was no escape.

America was compromised.

The wall was a masterpiece, not because of any aesthetics or innovative reason, but because of the sheer speed at which it was built.

Beyond Hermosillo in the west to San Antonio in the east, from coast to coast, the wall stretched over a distance of 16,000 kilometres.

But the cost of building the wall further south (where the distance between the east and the west coast was shortest), was too high in terms of the human life that might have to be sacrificed along the north side of the wall.

Every possible resource in the world was deployed along that thin line between USA and Mexico.

Large airplane carriers magically arrived via sea in a matter of hours. There was a barrage of large transport airplanes from the get-go. And long convoys of gigantic chrome trucks could be seen everywhere on the horizon.

Building a wall of that magnitude was a daunting task indeed. It began with drilling deep holes inside the dry desert soil. Then large concrete posts were slammed into these holes by gigantic, larger than life machines. It was as if god himself had come down from heaven and in a matter of hours, built something so monstrously big. The wall was almost as thick, as it was high.

Nobody was allowed to cross over from USA to the other side. Once built, every soul who had contributed to the building of the wall was retained on the other side.

There were towers and turrets where the troops had positioned themselves. The area north and south of the wall had been cleared of all civilians in case carpet bombing became necessary.

A similar wall was built between USA and Canada. It stretched beyond Vancouver in the west to Thunder Bay in the east.

The leaders from across the world didn't want to take a chance. The outbreak that had started with one rat bite, was spreading throughout the continent uncontrollably.

The wall was the world's biggest defence against the zombies. It had to be ready before the zombie horde arrived. And it was.

The world began to feel a little secure. A half-hearted evacuation attempt was being made at the request of the American President. The evacuees were flown to a bunch of remote islands in the Bahamas. No aircraft carrying the evacuees was allowed to go further than that or fly over either the North Wall or South Wall, as the walls were now called.

America was quarantined, well-guarded and safe behind the high walls.

Evacuation was expected to be carried out at strategic locations in the United States. There were a few simple rules which the government followed while selecting each spot. No spot closer than fifteen minutes to either wall could be selected since there was a high chance that a chopper with zombies aboard may fly out of control and crash beyond either of the walls. Distance was critical, and evacuation points would be set far enough from the walls for the whole world to feel safe.

Because of the fact that only selected spots were chosen for evacuation, it was imperative for the Americans to find a way to reach an evacuation spot. But even if they reached the spot, they would have to wait for hours before it was their turn to leave.

Still, human nature is indefatigable, no matter what the odds. People would move towards these evacuation spots because they had no choice.

Evacuation had finally begun. Things were smooth for the first few hours until the young pilot, Alex decided to follow his gut and responded to a distress call from Texas, which was not an authorized spot for evacuation.

It was around 1 a.m. when he took a chopper to Texas to rescue a family of five who were trapped on their terrace. He calculated it would take him an hour to get there from Atlanta. He checked if the fuel tank was full. And it was.

Alex finally decided to fly directly to the Bahamas after picking up his cargo and everything went as planned.

He met the distressed family briefly, and directed them into the chopper. But, just as he was about to take-off, the terrace door crashed open and a swarm of zombies came sprinting through. Two of them caught hold of the choppers rails just as it took off.

Alex tried to shake them off and succeeded after nearly crashing into a mobile tower.

The little girl, about the same age as the girl the sewer rat had bitten, spasmed and lay still on the floor.

"Throw her overboard," Alex shouted desperately. But the girl's family decided otherwise.

As the little girl came back to life, she attacked all the occupants of the chopper, without any discrimination or hesitation. The pilot was not spared either. As a result, the chopper careened out of control; its tail spinning frivolously as it flew south and crashed over the wall.

It landed in a mess of twisted steel and flame, a few miles south of the wall.

The military approached the crash site with extreme caution. They found the pilot and the four members of the family, charred to death. But there was no trace of the little girl. The girl had transformed; she was not little or an ordinary girl anymore. She was a zombie now.

The chopper had crashed at 2:31 a.m. It had been raining heavily. Aloof and separated from the pack, its instinct to survive had taken over her urge to infect. It made its way through the darkness, darting across the tight cordons of soldiers which closed the desert, straight into the suburb of Reynosa.

Reynosa was on high alert since the crash. There was a curfew in the area and the streets were riddled with soldiers.

The zombie lay low, crouching inside rain-filled gutters. It found its way to a small garden which belonged to the house at the end of the road. There it came across an unlocked cellar entrance and entered it.

Slowly, it moved through the basement towards the door at the top of the stairs, which led into the house. The door was open. It peeped into the living room. The room had quaint chairs which surrounded a large table.

The white-haired man Paul, whose daughters had long since moved away, was watching television. He was retired from work and lived with his wife Lynda who was in the kitchen at the time.

The zombie sneaked up behind Paul who had his back towards the door of his living room. He was busy munching popcorn from a bowl that rested in his lap.

He probably thought it was Lynda, nuzzling him from behind till the zombie took a bite of his neck.

He spasmed and died instantly.

Lynda entered the T.V. room a few seconds later, only to see her husband's dead body on the couch. The bowl of popcorn was upturned all over the upholstery and the floor.

Lydia was quivering with fear. She was about to call 911 when she turned on instinct and found the little zombie girl behind her, looking at her with yellow but lucid eyes. The girl's lips and chin were stained dark maroon with blood.

Within seconds, Lynda was struggling with the zombie whose teeth tore off the dress from her right shoulder blade. She held the blood drenched teeth at bay with her bare hands. The dignified old woman lay on the floor as she kicked and punched the little girl who clung to her, inching her way ever closer.

And then things got worse. Lynda was horrified to see Paul, who was alive again. She could recognise his shadow. But he was one of them now. Paul turned his eyes on her, a frightening yellow, and with reptile like agility, jumped at Lynda who lay on the floor, holding back the little girl.

Lynda had no chance. She watched in horror, both hands locked around the little girl as Paul, her husband of forty years, held her arm down and bit into it with all the force he could muster. Lynda shouted in pain and horror. Then there was silence. And two minutes later, Lynda woke up. The three of them chose to split up and discreetly merged into the dark night.

The three zombies kept to the side of the road and padded along at a good pace. They moved quickly and nimbly, eyes focused on one task and one task alone. To infect.

As they moved further south, they entered the more populated town of Monterrey.

In any kind of war, sacrifices, however useless, must be made.

Charles didn't know this. He had been a president of peace and profit. The threat of war had been ever present, but had mostly been created by the president himself.

A scared population is a docile population. He had remained in power well past his term, thanks to an amendment to the constitution. The people needed him. They were sure they did. But now that he was in the middle of a war, one which he hadn't started, he had no idea how to deal with it.

He had been evacuated immediately and been taken to Denmark where all the leaders of the world had assembled on short notice.

They were sitting around a spacious conference table, the size of a bus. Most of the seats were unoccupied but all the people who mattered were present.

"It's damned well impossible. Public sentiment won't allow it," said the representative from India. He was speaking in response to Charles' plea for evacuation.

"To hell with public sentiment! Humanity is at stake," roared Charles, looking around the table, daring anyone to oppose him.

His eyes fastened on Hung Ti, the Japanese Premier. Hung Ti was a short man who had never been known to utter a harsh word. But he was still acknowledged as one of the most powerful men in the world.

There were no representatives from the South and Central American countries.

Chairman Zedong, the Chinese Premier, was extremely reticent. Clearly, everyone wanted a sanction on the rescue operations out of America.

"It's the only way, we cannot risk a worldwide infection," said Chairman Zedong.

"Not even a single person," interjected the Japanese Premier, as if he knew what the American President was about to say.

Charles glanced at his British counterpart for support. Unfortunately, he found none.

Prime Minister Tom refused to meet Charle's gaze. Tom sat with his head bent low, staring at the glass of water and plate of cookies which lay in front of him, along with a thick file.

By and by he picked up the glass of water and took a sip.

"Too risky," he murmured, in a voice which only he could hear.

The problem was that no one had ever before seriously considered the possibility of a zombie attack. Hence nobody was prepared. No amount of politics and bickering would get them out of this situation.

The unexpected had happened and nobody had even the teensiest idea as to what to do about it.

But the problem of evacuation was simply a matter of time. Once the killer virus was released, there would be no threat anymore.

And that was where the Swiss Premier, De Gaulle came in.

De Gaulle was a tall, balding man with bushy eyebrows and thick lips which he constantly licked when nervous.

"A virus, gentleman, which causes such an extreme muscular reaction that the subject will disconnect his spinal cord from his brain in a matter of minutes."

The representatives had already been briefed by their aides, who had also already been briefed by the top scientists from around the world.

The thick file in front of each of them contained all the fruits of the research that had been carried out, fastidiously and with utmost urgency, in the past few hours.

It contained every possible scenario that could be imagined. The one that interested Charles was where a cure was found for the virus.

This scenario itself was divided into two parts.

The first part dealt with a situation where people could be made immune to the zombie virus.

The second part, which Charles found infinitely more useful for his case in favour of evacuation, was where the cure could reverse the zombie symptoms.

The chances of this happening had been calculated as 76,321 to 1; against.

There were many reasons that had been given to back this frightening number.

The primary one was that it was impossible for the zombie virus to be separated from the body.

The tests, which had been carried out in the Bahamas, where a zombie had been taken, had shown that the zombie virus attached itself to the neurons of the brain.

It infected each and every cell in a matter of seconds. And the chances of separating even a single cell once this bond was formed were extremely low; even lower than the number which had been posted.

"How long for the antidote to take effect?" Charles asked. He was talking about the antidote to the killer virus.

"Instantaneously, if administered by a syringe," answered Dr. Hawthorne, the head of the Center for Disease Control and Prevention, one of the leading public health institutes in America.

The air inside the room was muffled with uncertainty. No matter how assertive the American President was, as much he wanted the allies to support him during these testing times, the other representatives did not want to risk the life of the citizens of their respective countries.

"There will be no evacuation, not until next year. Only when we are satisfied, we will send our own teams to find survivors and rescue them," replied Hung Ti. He was gentle, as if he were talking to a child.

Charles nodded, tongue-tied. He felt helpless and knew that they were right. If he was to step in their shoes, he would have suggested, rather ordered, the same directive.

Plans to air-drop food, weapons and more importantly, the vaccine were being drawn actively.

"So far, the outbreak is restricted to America. At most, this is a freak occurrence which will not be repeated anywhere else. In that case, we must contain the situation immediately," said Hawthorne.

"We cannot take a risk. Not even with a single infected human," repeated Hung Ti.

Tom, the British Prime Minister nodded in assent.

Charles nodded too, like a soldier standing in the middle of a losing battle, wondering why he was there in the first place.

And, it was decided.

The Americas would be sealed off.

For one whole year.

The precise time at which America would be fumigated with the virus was pondered over in great detail.

The timing of each wave was critical. Moreover, the antidote should reach the citizens beforehand and allow them to vaccinate themselves before the first wave struck. The biggest hurdle was getting access to the antidote. The fact that most citizen were trapped in their houses, and could not even walk up to their front yard, posed a serious threat to the whole strategy.

How would they reach the vaccine, their bleak but only means of survival?

Undoubtedly, there would be a number of people who wouldn't make it to the vaccine and die an intensely painful death.

The only objective now was to ensure that the killer virus would murder only in the rarest and most unforeseen of cases.

There would be a series of twenty waves of fumigation. The entire country would be subjected to the colourless, odourless virus twenty times. Although after the first wave, troops would be sent in and the antidote administered manually.

The frequency and number of waves was decided based on the fact that a single wave of virus could not reach all the zombies. The ones who were hiding underground, locked in houses or perhaps even inside the mountain caves could possibly survive the lethal wave. The world could not take a chance.

There was a bigger risk which stared at them. If a zombie infected an immune human, someone who was injected with the antidote, there would be an immune zombie to put down. Hence it was decided that the city would be sprayed with different strains of the killer virus.

There was no time to be lost. With every passing second, more and more people were being killed in their homes, restaurants, parking garages, subway stations… wherever people thought they were safe and could find shelter.

But people should also have time and access to the antidote before the exercise began.

Finally, based on a complex matrix of factors such as when the region was infected and topography, airdrops and fumigation were scheduled.

The schedules were communicated to the American masses through radio/television, pamphlets dropped by planes and announcements on loudspeakers which penetrated every corner of the continent.

Later it was discovered that loudspeakers attracted the attention of zombies, making them more active. The practice had been discontinued ever since this fact was revealed.

No expense was spared. Every area was bombarded with the antidote at least twice with the hope and intent to make it accessible to the entire population.

The package was very easy to use, even for someone who didn't know how to read or write. It was a bright white rectangle, approximately half a foot in length, about three inches wide and two inches thick. It was made of strong cellulite which would decompose by itself after one week, if unused. This was keeping in mind that the ground would soon be littered with such drops and when the time came to drop the antidote to the modified strain of virus, people should not inject themselves with the antidote to the wrong strain.

The small rectangular compartments of the package contained four inoculation syringes, packed in a two by two arrangement. They were fastened in styrofoam and lined with dry ice and two tourniquets. A leaflet with a four-frame diagram explained that they were to be delivered intravenously.

Besides the antidotes, food was an essential prerequisite for humans' survival. To avoid confusion, food and weapons were air-delivered in distinguishing packaging. Food and weapons were packed in green and black colours, respectively. The weapons packed contained a shotgun, a short six-gauge device along with a simple user-training manual. Radios and emergency lanterns were also dropped intermittently.

The US government was in contact with a small section of the population but the majority it seemed were without means of communication, or worse, had been attacked and were now the attackers.

The movement of solitary zombies was being tracked by satellite. This data was being analysed by more than a million scientists across the world. The scientists were working in groups comprising anything from five to a hundred, all governed by a centralized group.

The entire world had united under this common peril.

According to the plan, the troops were instructed to enter the city only after the first wave of viruses was released. This would take a period of two days.

The release of the first virus was scheduled for 6 a.m. on Monday, 5 August 2017.

The modest bungalow was passed-on to the brothers by their father. The younger one of the two brothers shared the ground floor with their father when he was alive. Now, without his dad around, he had the entire house to himself and his family. He and his wife had three children, two girls and a boy.

He had always wanted a boy. When his wife gave birth to two girls, separated by a couple of years, they tried again, with the hope of having a son, and at the risk of having a third daughter.

So obviously, their son was the centre of their world.

Meanwhile, the elder brother, Quentin, had constructed one more floor atop the bungalow for his own family. The erstwhile bungalow was now a two-storey apartment building with two very large apartments.

Sebastian was at home on the day of the outbreak. He was pacing his room and listening to music. He had recently quit his job and decided to stay unemployed. To kill time, he preferred hashish.

He seldom watched TV, but was addicted to Facebook.

He saw the first post while he paced up and down.

Petra Krause: "Help me! I'm trapped at Stillwater Public Library. Zombies are running everywhere. This is not a joke."

He didn't react at first. Petra was a cute girl at his previous office. She had a penchant for taking selfies. Perhaps this was a joke, a gimmick to attract attention. It didn't seem funny. Not even original.

He checked the rest of his news feed.

"Help us! We don't know for how long the doors will last. If you are listening, do something!"

That was his friend's mother who lived alone near the university. She taught Sociology and was not easily excitable. In fact, it was impossible for someone of her nature to participate in what looked like a digital flash mob.

He scrolled further down.

Someone had taken a snap from the ground floor window of their apartment. The picture showed a street lined with houses. The street was full of people; people who were walking in the same direction, alert and agile, with a sense of purpose and affirmation. The crowd was dominated by men, followed by a few women and a couple of children.

A frantically-pacing Sebastian was now sitting in his chair with a blank stare, as if he were in a trance.

His room was on the west side of the first-floor apartment. The door of his room opened up in the drawing room where the television set was kept.

Sebastian went into the drawing room and turned on the TV. The Facebook feeds flashed inside his head. He felt a nameless spine-chilling fear piercing his bones, even though the afternoon was sunny and warm.

In a hurry, he opened the channel guide. All the news channels were stacked up on the right-hand side of the screen. He placed the cursor on the first one and previewed. It was Fox News, the national news channel.

The preview box popped-up on the left side of the screen and showed policeman firing at a crowded street, indiscriminately.

There was an eeriness about the crowd. Sebastian could sense it among the people who were running towards the police barricade. Before Sebastian could infer any further, the video on the screen was swapped with a studio background with a news anchor in front.

Sebastian clicked on the Fox News tab and the fifty-two-inch TV screen zoomed-in to the scene at the studio.

"The zombie outbreak, it is being called," the news anchor announced in a crisp, clear tone. "People in Oklahoma are advised to lock their houses and stay indoors where these zombies cannot get in. So far, these zombies are without weapons and cannot break down doors and windows. Help will reach you. The outbreak which started in Stillwater is spreading outwards. So far, no other outbreak has been reported. Please do not try to run and stay indoors. Lock your doors and windows…"

Sebastian looked outside through the large windows on his left. The drawing room was connected to a large sitting room facing south. The sitting room had a large empty space with a few chairs. The two big windows, also facing south, opened into a balcony which overlooked the garden.

Led by a hunch, Sebastian walked up to the balcony doors and opened one.

The commotion sent him back, reeling.

Floating along the warm summer sun and a hot, humid wind, the noise coming from across the street was jarring to the ears. Doors were being slammed, cars were jammed and honking on the otherwise secluded street that lay beyond the garden.

It seemed as if all of Oklahoma had come to see his neighbourhood.

A chopper passed overhead. He walked to the edge of the balcony and with one hand gripping the rail, leaned his head out.

On his left, he could see his neighbour; a second cousin and a childhood friend.

"Matt!" he shouted.

Matt lived in a bungalow, which had been converted into a three-storey apartment; it abutted Sebastian's first floor apartment.

He was standing in his driveway and loading suitcases in his

Volkswagen SUV.

"Matt," shouted Sebastian again, waving frantically.

Even through the commotion, Matt could not have missed hearing Sebastian. His driveway was only a few metres from where Sebastian stood.

Matt finished loading the suitcase inside the car. He turned and gestured towards a domestic help to open the gates. Only after that did he walk towards Sebastian, who was still waving frantically from his balcony on the first floor.

"Hi," said Matt, his expressions were that of a man who preferred not to be interrupted.

Sebastian ignored his expression and asked him, "Where are you going?"

"To the north," Matt gestured somewhere behind Sebastian, "towards New York, then Canada if I must. Where the lands are still free of these things."

Sebastian considered his choices. Matt had a plan. A plan to take his family away from death, as far as possible.

"The news channels are making announcements, urging us to stay inside," continued Sebastian.

Matt rolled his eyes at Sebastian, not for the first time in his life. "I'm off. You can do what you want," he said.

With that he walked back to his car. His wife, Hillary, a slender pretty woman, a few yours younger to Sebastian, came out of the house with a six-year-old girl prancing around her legs.

Sebastian went back inside the house.

The TV was flashing a map of the city. There was a red coloured circle with its centre at Hester St. It stretched all the way up north to the University and south towards Teal Ridge.

As Sebastian watched in horror, the circle expanded even further.

"This is the current rate of expansion," the TV anchor said, but Sebastian had already done the required mathematics.

His phone rang. It was his father.

"Hello," said Sebastian, glad to hear the familiar voice of his father.

"We are coming home... your mom, sister and I. We are in the car and heading home via McElroy. Is everything okay?"

"Yeah Dad," Sebastian found himself replying. "I'm just about to lock all the doors and windows."

"Good. Don't open the door for anybody. We'll be there in twenty minutes."

"Any traffic?" asked Sebastian. He wanted to listen to the voice on the phone for a little longer.

"No. It's quite the opposite. The streets are deserted."

"People over here are leaving for the north."

"Let them. You stay put."

"Okay," replied Sebastian, still on autopilot, and hung up.

He looked at his watch.

1:14 p.m., Thursday, 3 August.

He was caught in a surreal world in which clouds of thunder and lightning were gathering beyond the horizon. He could almost touch them.

His gaze drifted back to the news channel. The red circle drawn on Stillwater had further increased in diameter.

Sebastian went back to his room. He switched his computer on, typed 'zombie outbreak' and hit the search button.

The second hit showed him what he wanted. A software which would convert any given coordinate into time. He could estimate the time of breach by the first wave of the infected population.

Sebastian entered his address. The map zoomed-in, displaying his location. He looked at the time stamp, blinking in red.

6:45 p.m., Thursday, 3 August.

He had less than six hours to prepare. He went back to the first hit on Google. It was a website set up by the government and had everything you might need to survive the coming few days in America. He clicked on the link to open.

It was temporarily out of service.

He went back to Google. He felt a surge of adrenaline course through his veins. A feeling of restlessness soon followed.

He looked at his window and back at his computer screen.

The third and fifth hits were two popular news channels.

The fourth hit was a leader board where people who had encountered zombies could weigh-in.

Sebastian got up and walked towards his balcony.

Outside, the bustle still continued. Most people were packing and heading further north, away from the outbreak.

But some of them did choose to stay back.

His immediate neighbours to the right were examining the house, as though for the last time. They were a family of six people – grandfather, grandmother, mother, father and two children – along with and two servants who had served them for fifteen consecutive years now.

Their driver had also joined them with his wife and kid, making a total of nine people seeking shelter in the house. He was a sturdy fellow who drove his own Harley Davidson on the days he had an off. He was surely an asset to the family if it came to a fight, thought Sebastian as he watched them prepare for the coming onslaught.

Another chopper passed overhead.

Sebastian looked at his watch. Fifteen minutes had passed since he had spoken to his parents. He was still partially numb. But he knew that once this feeling had passed and he was in the midst of action, he would regret the time which he had spent idle.

He should also prepare. But what could Sebastian do besides

bolting all the doors and windows and hoping for the best!

The nearest market was a few hundred metres from his house, towards the south. The other one was a little further, to the north. But he had no plans to visit them. People would probably have plundered and looted them. But, as an afterthought, he realised that the suddenness and harshness of the outbreak had left people horror-struck. They could not afford to lose time on loots or rampages.

As far as provisions went, Sebastian was confident that they had enough to last them a month, if not a whole quarter. Such was the daily consumption in a house as large as his, that by saving on the daily waste alone, they could survive for months. At least that's what his calculations forecasted.

The stores were filled with biscuits, chocolates, that would keep them going for long. A trip to the supermarket was unnecessary at this point of time, he convinced himself. If truth be told, Sebastian had a bad feeling about venturing out of the house, towards the market. What if something happened, like he was attacked, and never made it back home?

1:31 p.m. His parents should be reaching soon. Meanwhile, he thought of something he could do to prepare for the coming night. Finally, he decided to take a walk south towards the market and gather a sense of things. If things looked orderly, he would go inside and buy provisions.

He went out the door of his first-floor apartment, locking it behind him, and began to climb down the stairs.

He had just stepped out of the gate when he saw the chauffeur-driven BMW of his parents coming down the west-end of the road. He opened the gate and the car made its way through to the driveway.

Like most of the houses in the city, this too had no garage. But it had a long driveway which passed a verandah to the right. The driveway further led past a small door on the right and ended just before the back lawn started.

The chauffeur parked the car at the very end of the driveway and got out. He lived further up north and Sebastian assumed he would head there soon after, to protect his wife and children.

His father was now shaking the driver's hand as he obstinately refused to help the Parkers any more than he already had.

Sebastian saw a great deal of cash changing hands as the chauffeur took off. He caught the driver at the gate.

"There is an app…" he began, but the chauffeur, Virender, cut him off.

"I know, I know," he nodded and slipped out of the gate.

Sebastian turned to see that his parents and his sister were unloading groceries and provisions from the car.

"Guns?" asked Sebastian, hopefully.

"Yes, revolvers," replied his dad. "And four shotguns."

Sebastian was gripped by a sensation that he was in a dream. He stepped towards the car.

"The stores are still functioning," said his mother, hauling a carton of baked beans.

"Mostly, people don't know what to do," added his father.

Sebastian helped them carry the provisions to the first floor.

"What about people who don't have proper shelter?" he asked, as his dad led the way up the staircase.

"Who knows? The government will probably think of something," replied his father.

His sister made an impatient noise behind him. Sebastian ignored it.

Unlike his sister, he had refused to join the family business. So far, he had switched careers from economics to advertising, with little success across the spectrum of his choice of careers. Living with his parents had given him the kind of confidence that even those who make it big in life did not have.

"Let's lock up," his father said once they had unloaded all the provisions from the car.

"I'm wondering why Heather or Marie haven't called up yet.," said Sebastian as he went down with his father to lock the main gate and the two consecutive doors which led to their house.

Heather and Marie were the two sisters that lived in the house downstairs. Their younger brother Dave, who would otherwise be at work at this time, had a fractured ankle and thus, was confined to the house.

Sebastian was surprised as he had heard nothing from him either. Nor had he heard from his busybody aunt, who lived on the ground floor, or his inept uncle who was married to her.

Marie and Heather were married and lived in different parts of the city. Marie was the eldest of the three siblings and lived in Sunset Park, the area which was already overrun by the outbreak.

"Your uncle and aunt are already indoors," Laura, Sebastian's mother replied at length. "Heather has locked herself inside her apartment in Lakeview. She was debating whether to come up to Rogers Drive or not, but your dad advised against it," she said, as they entered through the apartment door. She went to the right towards the balcony door to bolt it and checked if the windows were latched.

Pat, his sister was unwrapping the guns. Sebastian looked at her with interest.

"As if Marie and Heather would call you, to involve you in their decisions," she said to him in a tone which reeked of condescension.

She pulled out the shotgun and felt its barrel, its grip, almost lovingly.

"Do you know how to use that?" Sebastian asked, though he knew neither she nor him, nor anyone in their family had ever fired a gun or knew how to do so.

"I will," she replied, aiming the shotgun at the window abutting the balcony door.

The window was made of toughened glass and covered the drawing room from the south side. It extended from the ceiling till about the height of a five-year-old.

"Careful! Don't you shoot at the glass!" exclaimed Sebastian, in a mock alarm. Though it indeed was sound advice.

"We need to get some practice," said Pat.

"We all need practice," butted in his mom, as she went about checking and double checking every window and door.

"So what of Marie, then?" asked Sebastian.

"Haven't you heard?" replied Pat, opening the box of shotgun shells, balancing a grim smile on her face. "Nobody could get in touch with her or the kids." Then, she said, "Is anybody keeping an eye on the news?"

There was an unexpected excitement in her voice.

After looking around and pondering for a few seconds, Sebastian said, "You know, that oak tree overlooking the terrace is our worst enemy."

The tree he was talking about grew in the back lawn. It wasn't really a lawn because it was all cemented over. Many years ago, it had been a cowshed, but after Sebastian's grandfather passed away, nobody would take care of the cows. The sheds had to be torn down. This left the old tree stranded. There was a high boundary wall that separated the sprawling house behind them, from their own.

The tree grew straight and strong, spreading out its branches on the terrace, above the first floor. As a child, Sebastian had often debated climbing the tree to reach the terrace sans the stairs.

Right next to the window of Sebastian's room, to the west, ran the driveway.

The driveway cut perpendicular to the street outside, Rogers Drive. The road ran east to west and vice versa. The driveway was guarded by a large gate. It ran from the gate, northwards, past the verandah steps, towards the door which led to the staircase through which the first-floor apartment could be accessed, and to the back of the house where the oak tree rested.

If the zombies made their way through the door that led to the first floor apartment, they would hit a narrow passageway which spanned a few metres.

At the end of the passageway, there was a door that led to the ground floor of the bungalow. This door was always locked.

On the left to the door, there was a little landing. There was room enough for four people to stand, if they cramped close together. The landing led to the staircase which ran up and west before it turned back east, all the way to the front door of the family of four, who were presently preparing for the attack. An attack which was inevitable.

Sebastian's watch showed 2:21 p.m.

A little over four hours to go. Every nerve in his body was tense. The family was about to go on the terrace to practice shooting the guns.

They had purchased plenty of blanks too for them to practice and get accustomed to the heft and feel of the weapons.

They took the stairs that led from the drawing room, a single flight, to the terrace door, which was also made of toughened glass, like the balcony door.

Laura took the lead, carrying the two boxes of blanks, one for the shotgun and one for the Smith and Wessons. She also carried two boxes of live rounds, one for the shotguns and one for the Smiths.

Next came Quentin, the patriarch. He carried the two shotguns. He was followed by Pat, who carried two of the Smith and Wessons, one shiny black and the other a dull silver.

Sebastian came in the end, carrying a set of targets that came with the revolvers. They were square sheets of paper, with a shaded body of a human being. There were concentric circles in the centre of the paper-man, the kind which one finds in a shooting gallery. He also carried a hammer and some nails with him.

Laura unlocked the door and stepped outside. The mouth of the staircase opened towards the west, a few short paces to the wall that overlooked the driveway. Laura moved towards her right, went along the glass structure that housed the staircase, and stopped in front of the giant room that had been constructed atop the terrace. This room housed a table to play Table Tennis and a makeshift gym.

This room, which started from the north-west corner of the terrace, ran southwards and eastwards along the boundary, took up one-third of the space on the terrace.

Laura passed the narrow diagonal space between the TT room and the housing for the staircase, and stood in the moderate space between the TT room and the east wall of the house, the wall which was a part of Matt's apartment on the second floor.

It was a high wall, about ten feet tall. Behind it was Matt's daughter Radha's room.

It was this wall that Laura now faced.

"Hang them here. This will make for a good practice field," she told Sebastian, gesturing towards the high wall in front of her. To her left, i.e. to the north, stood the old oak tree and to her right was the steep fall to the garden.

Sebastian walked up to the wall and began hammering in the targets.

"But that's too close," said Pat.

"That's how close they'll be when you shoot them," said Quentin, leaving his sentence hanging in the coming darkness.

The TT room and the high wall were only about five metres away from each other. Close, as Pat had pointed out to her mother before.

They started practising with blanks.

Sebastian went first. He picked up the silver Smith and Wesson. He pressed a button and the magazine came out loose. His father Quentin silently opened the box marked 'blanks' and passed him the ammunition. Sebastian loaded the gun till it was full. There were nine rounds in all. Then he carefully lifted the gun and brought it up to eye level. "It's heavier than it looks," he said.

"It'll be heavier still, even more so, when you use live rounds," commented his father.

Sebastian disabled the safety, pulled the trigger gently and the world exploded.

For a second, his senses registered nothing. Then he realised his ears were paining from the loud bang and his wrist was hurting from the recoil.

The air was heavy with the smell of gunpowder. He looked around to see how his family reacted.

They appeared as numb as he was, since they too were in close proximity of the gunshot. Sebastian shook his head to clear it, and then turned towards the wall to fire the second shot.

This time he registered the recoil and the sound. He fired the entire magazine, trying to keep his gun level with the target, throughout the practice session.

"That's not so hard," he said as he stepped back.

The sharp sounds of gunshots were loud and darted across long distances. Other people were practicing too. The ones who had planned to stay inside their houses and wait for help to come, like the Parkers had done.

The homeless were among the first ones to arrive. Driven from street corners, bridges and railway stations, they came pouring into the streets, heading north, south, east; trying to outpace the zombies.

They were dangerous for they could break down windows and doors, leaving spaces for the zombies to squeeze through later.

Quentin clutched the shotgun between his hands, with the stock resting on the ground, between his legs, and prayed with his eyes closed. He wanted this sudden infiltration to stop.

But the homeless were not keen on stopping. They realised that once they broke into a habitation, others would soon follow, others of an undead variety.

So they kept moving. They had faith that the government would have made some provision for them.

The sounds of footsteps grew louder. Rogers Drive, the street on which Sebastian's house stood, was not part of thoroughfare. To get there, one would have to turn left from the main road that ran a ring around Stillwater.

The footsteps grew louder. The thud of their steps in unison was beginning to seem unbearable while they passed down Perkins Road. Rogers Drive remained isolated.

The city was soon consumed by another whiff of silence. This one even more uncertain than the one before. The sun was setting and the sky was a mix of grey and black. A few birds still flapped their tired wings, but soon, they too would retire for the day to rest.

And then an awful screeching howl echoed through the evening. The scream died down after a few seconds, but left the Parkers shocked and weak inside their hearts.

They could feel the evil, the air thick with fear and restlessness. And it did not stop. Just after the sunset, another painful shriek shook the evening with terror.

They were coming. The ruthless harbingers of death were coming.

Sebastian shivered as he wondered what it would be like for the homeless with no walls and toughened glass to protect them. How vulnerable they were, out on the streets, being followed by those… horrific sounds in the dark.

So far, all the information he had on these creatures, was sent by those who were trapped inside their houses. This included pictures and videos. In the videos, zombies were hunting; they were alert and predatory. Sebastian wondered what happened once the zombie spotted its prey. What would the frenzy look like?

He was sure he could fend off a small boy, or an old woman. But it would certainly be difficult to escape or kill a hefty infected male, in the throes of a frenzy.

Sebastian stared into the darkening sky and found the old whimsical and surreal feeling descending upon him.

A precursor to unbearable pain and carnage, Sebastian thought to himself, trying to rush back to reality and focus on the grim situation at hand. He hoped they were well prepared for the attack.

The use of guns would be their last resort. Their use would signify that the situation was out of control, the beginning of the end.

Truth be told, if zombies broke into the house, his family would not be able to keep them off for long, guns or no guns.

The Parkers had turned off the lights as a precaution. The light of the setting sun filtered through the big window in the drawing room. The Parkers got whatever little hope from that dim ray of the dying light. The street was well lit and the family could clearly see the road from their vantage point on the first floor. They crouched in one of the darker spots in the living room, near the south-facing windows, to ensure that they weren't spotted if the zombies happened to gaze in their direction.

The frequency of screeching and howling had increased. It engulfed the air and weighed on the family. The inhuman nature of the sound, the fear it created, the tension it pushed deep into the nerves, made it impossible to think.

Sebastian sat half paralysed. He prayed to every god he had disbelieved in. All he wanted was a little more time. Time to explore the world. Time to get married. Time to live. He remembered what it felt to live without the weight of an impending and violent death. The horrifying situation had compelled him to reflect upon the life which he had led so far. He wondered why he used to complain so much about nothing. If only, he wished, he could come out of this situation alive, he would be a changed man, more grateful while counting his blessings.

His thoughts were interrupted by the loud, repeated, screechings. The beauty of this beautiful moonlit evening was adulterated with the noise that shook the streets every now and then. Sebastian almost felt like laughing at the helplessness of the situation, their misfortune.

And then he heard one up-close. The scream sounded like it came from the east end of Rogers Drive. The bungalow the Parkers resided in was located close to the east end of the road. It was just two houses away from it.

A horrible, pitiful noise hung in the air for a few seconds and broke into a brief interlude thereafter.

Waves of menace flowed through Sebastian's body. His mind was jammed and his body was stiff with anticipation and fear.

This was it. No more thinking. No more planning. There was no time for emotions or prayers. It was now or never. Survival was the only priority.

The zombie on the east end of the road screeched again; louder and more insistent this time.

Sebastian wanted to cover his ears. He wanted to relax his body and relieve his bladder which was ready to burst.

Another screeching sound; this time from the west end of the street. And then Sebastian caught the first glance of a zombie which came from the east end of Rogers Drive. It was alert, watchful and made little bird like movements with its head as it walked.

It was a man; dressed in a tattered black suit, caked with mud and blood. Incongruously, the neck-tie was still intact.

It walked past the houses, bobbing its head and looking at each of the gates in turns. It was hard to make out the man's features in the collecting dusk, but Sebastian had his binoculars handy.

He took a good look at the zombie. He was bitten in the face and had his cheek ripped open. The blood had coagulated into an unhealthy mass which was now infected. Its hands were filthy, and bits of loose flesh, hair and cloth were hanging from its fingernails.

The man would have had a gaunt face once, with laugh-lines around the eyes. But he was not a man anymore. He would never laugh again.

The zombie paused outside the gate of the bungalow next to the Parkers'. The bungalow where Matt lived. It looked up and down the street in quick movements. Then it pushed the gate to test if it opened.

The gate didn't budge. It was bolted and secured by a gigantic lock.

The zombie pushed again and for all the headway it made, it might have been pushing a large block of concrete.

Sebastian waited with bated breath. The screeching sounds were becoming louder and louder. The zombie seemed unfazed. It knew what a gate was. It screeched once more and threw itself against the gate, more forcefully this time.

The sight looked more furious in the hazy darkness. The inhabitants of the bungalow were locked inside, scared to death.

The 'man' threw himself on the gate and screeched, made that gyrating, ear tingling, maddening sound. It sounded like a maniac laughing and a baby crying, both at the same place and time.

Before Sebastian could understand what had happened, the air exploded in a frenzy of sounds.

The scream was much louder than the first one. Sebastian was forced to cover his ears. They came like a pack of stray dogs – solitary, territorial and yet, part of one group.

Each one was alert and coordinated with the rest, without the need to utter a single word. Just those horrible screeches. The one who led the pack stopped and watched the zombie banging against the robust, immovable gate.

The others froze behind it. There were two women and three men.

They all tilted their heads, one way at first and then another. They were focused on finding humans and were immune to distractions. They were listening, smelling and watching.

Suddenly, the zombie in lead rushed forward and banged hard against the gate.

Its body hit the gate and it fell back on to the ground. The other zombies screeched and rushed towards the gate, each one banging against the gate in turn.

They were bleeding now from the injuries which the constant hammering on the gate had inflicted upon them. This had rendered them tougher and even more persistent.

Their screeching attracted more zombies.

One after another they came pouring from the east end of Rogers Drive and joined their counterparts.

Soon, there wasn't enough room for each zombie to hit the target. Sebastian's count had crossed thirty-five before he stopped and looked at the horde with a certain detachment.

Now the horde moved as one body, hitting the gate and falling back, then hitting the gate again. The gate swelled inwards each time the horde pushed against it and pivoted back outwards as it pushed back.

Sebastian could hear it groaning in protest as more zombies came and joined, their numbers burgeoning.

Sebastian said a silent prayer.

The other gates on the street including the Parkers' own stood still and deserted.

The zombies, it seemed, had united for a common pursuit.

It was a strange sight. Men, women, young and old... screeching and shaking the gate with boundless energy. They intended to kill every inhabitant inside the house and wouldn't rest till they hunted down and infected the last human being.

'Do I actually have a chance against this brutal and endlessly swelling horde?' thought Sebastian.

The gate was beginning to give in now as more zombies joined the horde. It rattled and began to buckle.

The night was full of screeches and the noise of twisting metal.

Sebastian would never forget the noise – the rattling of the gate, the screeching and howling, the loud thump of his heartbeat.

There was a loud crack and Sebastian watched in horror as the bolt gave way and the gate swung open.

The gates opened inwards and the zombie horde swarmed up the driveway and into the compound. They fell over each other as they spilled into the driveway in their excitement.

Sebastian watched as they swarmed around the neighbouring bungalow, screeching triumphantly, a victorious, inhuman sound.

They knocked against the toughened glass of the windows and beat themselves against the doors, excitedly searching for a way through.

Meanwhile, more zombies kept pouring in through the open gates.

A six feet high boundary wall distinguished the Parkers' residence from that of their neighbour's.

The edge of the wall had no spikes or cut glass. A young Sebastian had often complained about this. His father however was confident that the house was secure and paid no heed to his concerns.

All four members of the Parkers family watched petrified as the zombies began piling against the wall.

A tall and barefoot woman was wearing what had been a short top and a skirt once. She climbed up and grabbed the top of the boundary wall.

She screamed and pulled herself up.

And then the electricity went off.

The 'L' shaped drawing room ran parallel to the street outside. On either side of the drawing room, there were bedrooms to the north and the south. The bedroom facing north with windows overlooking the backyard belonged to his parents. The one facing south was the guest room which belonged to Pat, temporarily.

The bottom of the drawing room faced south which was where the sitting room was and where the entire family sat together to feel safe amid the madness and havoc wreaked by the zombies.

The kitchen was to the north of the drawing room, next to Sebastian's parents' bedroom. One could see the backyard from there. Pat's room, or the guest room while Pat was in college, was located to the south of the drawing room and was separated from the sitting room by the staircase which ran up to the terrace.

The zombies were unaffected by loss of electricity. But with the lights out, Sebastian realised that the last streaks of the sun had completely faded. The only light one could see was the bluish-white light of the moon.

And in the moonlight, he was terrified to see the female zombie scaling the wall. She jumped down the other side in one swift movement.

She crossed the garden, headed towards the verandah on the ground floor and kicked the large doors and screeched angrily.

Sebastian could not see what was happening around the doors of his neighbour's ground floor apartment. The balcony built in front of the south facing windows, where he sat now, blocked his view. If he wanted to find out more, he would have to take the risk and open the balcony doors to step out.

He could see more zombies crossing over the boundary wall. They were fearless and unstoppable.

Swift and completely consumed with what they were doing, they started banging the doors of the ground floor apartment which were right under Sebastian's house.

He had heard that sound of twisted metal and splintering wood before. The groaning of locks, bolts and hinges under immense pressure.

He listened in numb horror as the wretched door finally gave way to the blood-thirsty and unquenchable assault.

Besides the screeching and howling, Sebastian could hear gunshots. Loud and painful to the ears, but short-lived.

And then Sebastian heard it.

He could barely hear it at first. After a few seconds of concentration, he was sure of what the sound was.

It was a shrill sound, like a human screaming with pain. The sound was constant and terrifying. It felt as if a someone was being eaten alive.

The thought made him shiver with fear. He stood up, gripped with terror and panic. His head was spinning. All the windows of the house were closed. The hot and humid air circulating inside the house aggravated his pain and discomfort. Sebastian sucked in a lungful of the stale air, trying to regain focus.

"Sit down!" Pat ordered desperately in a loud whisper.

As Sebastian's head cleared, he realised he could now hear the screams from the window of his parents' bedroom. *From behind the house.*

He stumbled as he made his way to the kitchen, his mind still wandering in circles. And through the kitchen window, a large one that faced the north, he saw the devastation of the sprawling two-storey bungalow behind them.

The night had been chaotic, full of never-ending screams and animal sounds. The Parkers had ignored the continuous wailing that was all around them. During the last two hours, they had stared at the gate next to theirs, separated by a length of a garden, forgetting that the world around them was being inexorably invaded by zombies.

The bungalow behind their house was swarming with zombies. They were on the terrace balconies and sprawled all over the lawns.

The one-storey bungalow behind his house, which belonged to his neighbours, was massive as compared to the Parker residence. And the grounds that surrounded the bungalow were even larger, making the compound seem gigantic.

At least a hundred zombies had entered through the gate and occupied the huge plot, which was the size of four football fields.

The gate lay besieged, swinging on shattered hinges. It faced Perkins Road, the one with all the thoroughfare and had borne the brunt of the main section of the zombie army.

They were throwing themselves on the windows, doors and even the walls. They howled and screeched. Men, women and children alike. Fearlessly, they screeched and pushed against the doors and windows.

But the bungalow, with its toughened windows and hardened doors, similar to the Parkers' bungalow, had withstood their assault so far.

It was the strangest and the most terrifying sight Sebastian had ever seen.

He knew that the zombie horde would soon gang-up in front of the bungalow's main door, just like they had at his uncle's below him and would push it till it broke open.

In the light of the half-moon, Sebastian heard the loud tick of the inverter running on low batteries.

The loud tick which would end in a loud cry once the inverter batteries ran out completely, unless someone went and switched it off. The inverter was housed in a cabinet underneath the tall oak tree in the backyard.

Sebastian stared at the bungalow in front of him. It was swarming with zombies. No human would be spared.

And the same zombies would soon attack their bungalow. It was the next in line. Was this their fate? Would they die screaming and begging for their lives?

Turning the invertor off would hardly make any difference since they would be dead in a matter of hours. What difference would a few minutes make when the end was inevitable?

He finally left the scene taking place behind his backyard and went back to the drawing room.

Inside the room, he found his father standing next to the large west-facing windows of the sitting room which overlooked the driveway. Quentin was looking down at the driveway fearfully. Sebastian had never seen his father so terrified. Quentin had always had trouble in keeping himself composed during tough circumstances. He would break into the most frightful rages, assume the most childish of expressions at times and could be quite unfair of his treatment of others.

But he had never looked scared.

Laura was sitting where he had left her. Her head was buried inside her hands. She was crying.

Quentin's fearful eyes now looked at Sebastian.

"They're standing at the door," he said in a loud whisper.

The door he was referring to was made of solid oak and guarded the entryway to the first-floor apartment from the driveway. It led to a staircase which opened into the drawing room through another strong door made of solid oak wood.

"They want to get in," wailed Laura, with soft but honest conviction.

Sebastian turned to look at Pat. She was staring away into the distance, sightlessly.

Sebastian had no idea what to do.

It was 10:05 p.m. A mob of zombies had now collected at the Parkers' driveway. They made well-timed attempts to push the door hard and break through.

The oak resisted but made loud startling noises. Quentin reloaded his shotgun. Pat was holding on to her shotgun, arms tensed. She was standing in front of the door that opened from the staircase into the drawing room. This was their last line of defence.

The zombies still hadn't made it into the staircase. Quentin was still watching them push the driveway door.

Sebastian was pacing the drawing room steadily, trying hard to pacify his mind, to think straight. Laura was still sitting in the same place. She hadn't moved even once, a shotgun lay on the coffee table next to her.

Sebastian doubted if she would even pick it up. Not that it would do any good. There were too many zombies and the family had limited bullets.

Sebastian looked at the Smith and Wesson in his hand. The metal was cool and impersonal. He checked that the safety was off. The shotgun slung off his shoulder.

'This is it,' he thought.

And just as his thought faded, the driveway door crashed open.

The flight of stairs was not straight. They first ran to the west, towards the driveway and then double backed on themselves heading east and finally to the door of the drawing room.

The first thing that hit Sebastian was the smell. A dead rotting thing, as putrid as fresh garbage and as disgusting as human faeces.

Then came the sound. The screeching had sounded loud through the first-floor windows. But the screams, amplified to an unbearable level, inside the narrow confines of the stairwell, made Sebastian's otherwise tough knees buckle.

But for the large door in front of him, Sebastian felt like he was standing in a forest, stranded and surrounded by predators. It was as if human evolution had never taken place. That there was no safety or shelter.

The zombies must have made quick headway because even as the echoes of the crashing door were dying, the first zombie hurled itself against the front door of the Parkers' residence.

The door held, though all four Parkers recoiled involuntarily.

Then came the second and third impact. Another zombie joined the assault. The impacts came more frequently now. And they were growing louder.

Sebastian could sense the rage in their screeches. It looked as if some ancient virus had resurfaced and wanted to claim the earth as its own. As if all its hatred, vindictiveness and vengeance, which had been nurtured for millions of years was now unleashed.

The zombies were repeatedly banging against the door. No matter how hard the zombies tried, the narrow passageway could not accommodate more than three or four of them at one point of time. Which meant that the zombies could not get the same leverage they could apply to the driveway door, or the gate.

Their thuds against the door were becoming louder and more desperate. Like they were trapped and trying to get out. They were screeching sporadically. Their noise stank of frustration. They would find a way, like they always did. They just had to keep trying.

But for the moment, they were baffled.

Sebastian watched the front door in disbelief. He had thought his time had come. This was a second lease of life. Short-lived, but important.

The Parkers sat on the dining table at the far end of the living room with their eyes fixed on the front door.

Only Sebastian stood alone inside his parents' bedroom, watching the lavish bungalow behind their house slowly succumb to death.

The stairwells inside were broader and more spacious. The zombies were now tumbling out on the roof, on the balconies, looking for prey to feed on. They were bent on making sure that no one escaped alive.

Soon, they would be desperate to pounce upon the nearest prey, the Parkers.

A ten feet high wall stood between the overrun bungalow and the Parkers' backyard. The wall was covered in shrubs which made it easy to climb for a determined zombie.

What if the zombies came from that direction?

But then, no matter how many zombies they attracted, the passage leading to the front door would accommodate no more than four.

The only lacuna in the plan was the tree that stood tall inside Parker's backyard. The old tree had its branches siphoning all the way to the terrace.

If enough zombies climbed up that tree, they could easily force themselves inside through the terrace doors. A freak twist in architecture was protecting Parkers from the onslaught which was coming from the driveway. It would fail miserably if the zombies ransacked the terrace.

The terrace door was made of toughened glass, similar to the doors of the balcony. It would not withstand the violence for long.

Sebastian pushed these thoughts away from his head. The tension that had built up in the past couple of hours started leaking away. His mind had been whirring too fast for it to think coherently.

Sebastian's family had picked up a radio as part of the provisions made by the government. They needed to turn it on and find out what was happening in the rest of the country.

He brought it out from its casing and joined his distressed family, who were still glued to the dining table.

Through the front door of the drawing room, they could hear a vicious creak as zombies ripped apart one of their own. They had taken a break from their mission to barge into the front door and were now busy satiating their nauseating hunger.

Inside the drawing room, Sebastian could hear the sound of a cartilage being crunched on the other side.

It will soon be daylight. He wondered how will zombies react when they saw his family crouching in the drawing room through the glass windows.

Whatever happens, he thought philosophically, things will only get worse.

The information on the radio concurred with his prognosis.

The US government was using every radio station in Stillwater to make urgent announcements. The rest of the time, the radio gave out static. There were announcements on the density of zombies in different areas of the country. So far, the reports focused on Stillwater. The location of evacuation points was also broadcasted.

Everything was happening in slow motion. Too slow to survive, thought Sebastian.

The most interesting announcements were with regard to the

virus. After evacuating as many Americans as possible, the government would use biological warfare to exterminate the zombies.

They would also drop food and weapons for the humans, and of course, the antidote.

The drops would begin on 4 August.

There were similar announcements. The Parkers heard them all, till the radio started repeating them.

Quentin looked at Sebastian and beamed. Then he looked at Laura and Pat with his eyes full of satisfaction and relief.

But Sebastian thought otherwise. Stillwater would be fumigated in approximately twenty-four hours. That was too long a time lapse to survive when every zombie in the world wanted to enter your drawing room and shred you to pieces.

"Time is critical. They should begin with gassing immediately," Sebastian said to no one in particular.

"Have faith, little brother," said Pat, smiling at him condescendingly.

Sebastian closed his eyes and took a deep breath.

There was no wi-fi, no cellular network. The inverter's battery was still functioning. Truth be told, Parkers weren't using electricity. Not that it mattered anymore.

Sebastian felt trapped. Alive but trapped. The uncertainty of this whole situation had made him restless.

He went to the kitchen, and made himself a sandwich.

From the large window inside the kitchen, he could see the bungalow behind his house. Zombies were pouring in a line through the lawns and climbing the wall that separated his plot from theirs.

"Come, you bastards!" Sebastian said aloud. It made him feel better.

He sighed and went back to the drawing room.

Pat was checking the weapons. Sebastian hoped it wouldn't come to that. He did not want to use them.

Quentin and Laura were hunched over the radio. They had barely spoken after the attack had begun. It was hard for him to look at their glowing, joyful faces. The sombre radio announcements had given them new hope to survive. Sebastian observed them carefully as he munched the sandwich. It was tasteless inside his mouth.

There were a few zombies inside the garden in front of their apartment. They were crossing over to the driveway. Cautiously, Sebastian made his way to the west end of the drawing room and looked into the driveway through the large window.

He was horrified to see more than a hundred zombies within that crunched, confined space. They were all pushing forward towards the door in the driveway.

The unruly line entered the door and was lost to sight. The loud thumping to his right reminded Sebastian where the line ended. They were aggressive and without reason. The zombies would never give up.

Sebastian took a long, deep breath, thinking whether or not should he count them, purely for academic purposes. He didn't have the ability, he realised. He was dead tired. He finished his sandwich and stretched out on the floor. He closed his eyes for a second. In the darkness, the noises sounded worse.

The howling, the screeching, the thumping. With nothing else to focus on. Incessant. Relentless. Like a world was being torn to shreds. The world reduced to madness. His world.

He opened his eyes.

Someone had turned on the radio again.

'The evacuation will commence by chopper from points in Kansas, New Mexico and Arkansas. The points of evacuation in Kansas are as follows...'

Sebastian closed his eyes again and went to sleep.

He woke up, only to find himself being shaken roughly.

Sebastian was completely disoriented for about a second. He was lying in the drawing room. It was dark outside, except for the moon. Quentin was sitting next to him, whispering earnestly as he shook his shoulder.

And then he heard the noise. It had been playing somewhere softly in the back of his mind, somewhere in his dreams or in his subconscious mind. But in reality, it sounded much worse.

The screeching, the howling, and the thumping. And the smell. Again. He had been through the same disgusting labyrinth, just before sleep brought him temporary respite.

The night was alive with the undead. And with a rush Sebastian remembered what had happened.

"Wake up, they're dropping the antidote," his Dad was saying.

Sebastian, still lying prone on the ground, turned to look at his Dad.

He sat up and folded his legs underneath him.

His sister was sitting on the floor, next to his Dad. The radio lay between them. Laura was in the kitchen.

"They are announcing the schedule of the drops," said Pat.

"What drops?" asked Sebastian groggily.

"The antidote, silly."

Both Quentin and Pat were looking fresh, as if they had rested. Rested? Amid this ever-deteriorating situation. Sebastian wondered if they had actually gone and taken a shower.

"How do we get the antidote?" asked Sebastian. A thought had just crossed his mind.

Both Quentin and Pat stared at him in silence.

"How do we get to the antidote?" he asked again.

They sat and discussed the matter at length over a dinner of cold tinned baked beans with soft bread as they watched the first rays of daylight hit the sky.

Sebastian was stuck in a cycle of being indecisive. After every few minutes, his stomach would lurch, he would battle a feeling of shitting his pants, then get a few minutes of calm before he remembered his predicament, and then his stomach would lurch again.

The first wave of the antidote would be dropped at 6:00 a.m. that morning.

The second one was scheduled for 6:00 p.m. in the evening.

Oklahoma would be gassed at 6:00 a.m. on the following day, on 5 August. Similar schedules had been drawn for all the other states in America. In Kansas, which Matt should have crossed by now, the gassing would take place on 6 August. And so on.

All the result of a complex and reliable matrix, the radio made repeated announcements.

Sebastian looked at his watch. It was 4:45 a.m., Friday, 4 August.

He was worried about retrieving the antidote. His head was filled with different kinds of scenarios, some leading to success and victory, but most to a horrible and painful death.

If the antidote was dropped in the front lawns or the courtyard at the back of the house, the Parkers would have no chance to retrieve it.

The safest place for them to pick up the antidote was the balcony on the first-floor. But the terrace above the balcony killed the possibility of the antidote landing inside the balcony.

The terrace was their next best bet.

It was 5:45 a.m. Nothing had changed, except that the Parker family had hastily eaten a breakfast of cornflakes and powdered milk.

At 5:59 a.m., they heard the planes fly above them. By 6:01 a.m. they were gone.

The air was thick with parachuted antidotes. The sealed, rectangular boxes with life-saving drugs had finally arrived. The real challenge was to retrieve the antidote before it was too late. Sebastian hated this battle for survival, the survival which he had always taken for granted. He despised the gunshots, the screeches and the blood. But he had to fight. If not for himself, then for Laura, Quentin and Pat.

Sebastian could see the antidotes floating down from the brief patch of sky visible to him from the drawing room. The tiny white parachutes safely carrying them to the ground.

Death from the virus would be swift and painful. It had been chosen for its efficacy as a killing machine, he knew.

If only the antidote landed at the right place. A place which he could access and not be killed by zombies.

The parachutes drifted closer to the ground. Sebastian saw one floating past the window, overlooking the driveway.

"There's one in the courtyard," said Laura from the kitchen.

And that was all. Quentin had climbed up the stairs to the terrace, and had been watching the terrace through the glass windows which rendered a full view of the terrace.

He came down stairs, with a horribly dead and crestfallen expression on his face.

"There'll be another drop in the evening," said Sebastian in a flat voice.

They were now gripped by a new fear. They could hold out against the zombies somehow, but how would they escape the virus? The virus which would kill everyone living, human, zombie, or animal; it did not discriminate.

The two packages which contained the antidote lay where they had fallen. The zombies had completely ignored them. There was one lying on the driveway, a little away from the door that led to the staircase.

Sebastian could see that it was being trampled under hundreds of stomping feet. It would soon be completely useless. Not that anyone would ever be able to get to it.

The other package lay in the courtyard and was just as impossible to get.

There was nothing that Parkers could do. Except stay alert and wait for the next air-drop.

Matt's car rolled along easily for the first hundred kilometres or so. It was an old SUV but a reliable one.

Matt had seen a few broken-down cars on the interstate. He had ignored them and kept the car racing at the speed of eighty miles per hour.

The family had their meals inside the moving car. When he felt too tired to drive, his wife Hillary took over. Philip was next in line. They controlled the wheel in turns. Everyone besides Bridget, who didn't know how to drive.

The first traffic jam hit them around 5:30 p.m. It was on the outskirts of a small town north of Oklahoma. A truck had turned turtle on the road and a small passageway was available to move while it was being cleared. The traffic moved like a snail.

The narrow passageway permitted only one car to pass at a time. Naturally, it was choked by cars from different lanes, each outdoing the other in a display of haste and stupidity.

Matt slammed his hand on the steering wheel in exasperation. Hillary turned towards him and gave him a warning glance.

Radha was sitting with her grandparents on the rear seat of the car. Phillip was making her sing nursery rhymes while he made appreciative noises and encouraged her to recite more vividly, with expressions.

Radha had been told that some bad people had arrived from out of state and that the family was temporarily relocating to the nearest military base.

Even this much had put too big a strain on the six-year-old's mind. It had taken her hours to come to terms with this sudden discomfort, before she finally stopped crying.

Matt turned on the radio and adjusted the volume till it was audible.

The radio was giving updates on how far the zombies had been able to penetrate the American states. Besides that, it also announced updates on the evacuation drive, the virus and antidote schedule, tips and suggestions, among other things.

Matt drummed his fingers on the steering wheel. Despite Hillary's warning, he couldn't help it. He wanted to shout, to explode.

The world was coming to an end. Zombies in Stillwater! Too many books and movies had made him dead to the reality, to the real meaning of the threat to his life

He glanced to his left, at the car next to theirs. It was a Volkswagen Beetle belonging to an elderly couple. The woman sat behind the steering wheel, while the man was sleeping.

Matt wondered about the man who was asleep. How could he be so calm in a time like this? Perhaps they had less to live for.

The woman at the wheel turned towards Matt and smiled.

Matt smiled back at her, a little uncertainly. The woman then turned to look at Radha in the back seat and mouthed, "Good luck."

Suddenly Matt didn't feel as impatient as he had a few seconds ago. He felt rather relaxed.

Hillary had her iPad in front of her. "According to the Zombie Area Map," she said softly to Matt, "we have another twenty-four hours to reach the military base."

Hillary wanted to reach out and comfort Matt. The base was no more than a few hours away. But she knew that Matt was considering the unforeseen, a dangerous but necessary exercise.

What if they were ambushed? What if they got two flat tyres?

What if there were too many traffic jams and they had to walk?

Hillary harrumphed with impatience. Now like Matt, she was doing it too. She was worried. She was calculating the odds when she knew next to nothing. The government was trying their best, she told herself. If anyone had a chance in such a situation, it was the Americans.

She watched Matt while he listened to the radio intently. He was too engrossed with the radio to brood over the traffic jam. Hillary was relieved at the thought.

She turned around and smiled at Radha.

"Honey, tell grandpa about the poem we wrote," she said to Radha who had now forgotten all about the bad men who were chasing them.

"I want to pee," announced Radha.

The car was still stuck; the traffic was jammed. But Matt was strictly against anyone venturing outside the vehicle. He said it was too dangerous and made them vulnerable to the other biggest danger next to zombies, other people.

He tried to mollycoddle his daughter into waiting a few hours, but he knew she wouldn't understand.

A pretty pickle he was in.

"Papa," said Radha because Matt was behind the wheel, "I want to pee."

'Clever girl,' thought Matt.

There was no other option. One of them would have to take Radha to the side of the road.

Matt felt exposed. But, he realised, this was the most opportune time, if any, to leave the car. They were surrounded by people. Nobody would dare to hijack their car with so many watchful eyes all around.

Hillary was looking at him for confirmation. Matt nodded his head slightly.

"Ma," said Hillary, looking at Bridget. For one second, Bridget went pale. She thought Hillary was asking her to accompany Radha outside.

"Can you pass me Radha's bag?"

Bridget sighed. Her reaction did not go unnoticed. Hillary rolled her eyes as Bridget fearfully passed her the bag.

And then the traffic started moving. The jam had been cleared. More than eight traffic policemen manned the narrow passageway, but at least the traffic was moving.

Radha was the only person who was disappointed with the moving traffic.

"I have to pee," she repeated.

"I'll take out the jar," said Bridget triumphantly.

The digital clock on the dashboard showed 7:23 p.m.

They had been on the move for close to six hours now, at a stretch. The nearest evacuation point was five hundred miles away from their house. Just a little further, thought Matt.

The radio was telling them that the zombies were still more than half a day behind them. This meant that there was ample time to stand in line, board a chopper and be free of this terrible epidemic, thought Hillary.

It was at 7:45 p.m. when they saw their first chopper. It was heading west to east, which meant it was coming to pick up Americans.

By 8:00 p.m., the air was thick with them.

They finally approached the first barricade at the Kansas-Oklahoma border.

Flooded with confidence, Matt decided it was time to break a little ice.

"Who wants to see the Bahamas?" he asked Radha.

"I do," replied Radha instinctively.

Bridget ran a loving hand through her hair.

"We will be there very soon," she said, reassuring the little girl that her wish would be fulfilled.

"Just a few more metres and we'll be safe," said Matt.

Hillary barely paid attention. She was busy doing the math inside her head.

A round-trip between Kansas and the islands would take them around twenty minutes. If the choppers were together able to transport close to ten thousand people in a single journey, thirty thousand were expected to be transported within an hour. By this calculation, three hours implied that close to a hundred thousand people would be transported to the Bahamas.

Would their turn come before the zombies caught up?

Matt looked at his watch. It was 2:30 a.m. They were on a chopper headed towards New York.

Not all choppers were heading for the Bahamas. Some were headed north.

Once the country was fumigated, nobody would have to run and hide.

All people really needed right now, the local authorities had decided, was a bit of a head start.

Kansas, from where Matt and his family were taking off, would soon be a ghost town. The soldiers would be the last ones to leave.

The sound of gunfire in the background faded as the chopper headed north.

If they could outrun the zombies long enough till the virus was released, they'd be safe. The whole family had been inoculated against the virus at the airport.

According to the new schedule, New York would be sprayed with the virus on 6 August, 6:00 a.m., one day after Oklahoma.

The states in-between would be gassed earlier; the exact time would depend on their distance from the epicentre of the outbreak.

Matt closed his eyes. The decision to flee from Kansas was weighing him down.

He had taken a big chance. But staying put was not safe either. They would land in New York by 3:00 a.m. His family would finally be safe, away from the darkness of death.

He watched as the countryside disappeared underneath the chopper. They had crossed a few more cities. Any other time he would be sitting next to Radha and telling her which was which. He sat and stared forlornly at the scenery.

People up north were staying put. They had already inoculated themselves and were waiting for De Gaulle's virus to be released. They would never really know what the outbreak was about. Like him, they would never have to face or fight a zombie during their lifetime.

'With a bit of luck,' thought Matt, who was still calculating the odds.

He wrapped the blanket he had been given by the military officials around himself more tightly.

Radha was fast asleep, despite the noise. Hillary was busy watching the scenery and had an intrigued look on her face. Bridget and Phillip were talking to each other in hushed tones.

Everything seemed calm, peaceful and normal. For now.

Sebastian paced the drawing room. The clock did not tick for him anymore. Time no longer mattered. They were left with only one more chance to ascertain their survival.

Several other packages had been dropped, but Sebastian didn't bother. He was anxiously waiting for the air-drop which was scheduled for 6:00 p.m.

He glanced at his watch. It was 5:30 p.m. already.

He wished that he was somewhere else. That the zombie plague hadn't happened. He would give up anything for a cup of tea without this lingering fear of impending doom.

Quentin went up to the terrace. Laura stationed herself in the kitchen. Pat and Sebastian waited in the drawing room. Sebastian debated going onto the balcony so he could try to snag a floating package. But he decided against it. The chances of a package ever coming that close were slim. The likelihood of him getting spotted by a zombie almost certain.

That is when Quentin came downstairs.

"There's a zombie on the terrace." To be precise, the zombie was crouched on top of the shed that housed the TT table and gym.

As Sebastian had anticipated, the zombie must have climbed its way up the tall tree and made its way to the roof. And there it was, crouched atop the prefabricated shed which occupied the north-west corner of the terrace. It was presently crouched on the northwest edge, facing north and towards the tree.

A loud roar followed Quentin's announcement. The planes had arrived.

"Quickly," hissed Laura. "Places."

"Be very quiet," Sebastian told Quentin as Quentin turned to make his way up the stairs.

The planes roared past again and were gone in seconds. White parachutes littered the air. Sebastian waited with bated breath. This was it. Their only chance now to escape certain death.

One of the parachutes was lingering in the west. It floated closer and closer to the ground. It brushed against the balcony on the first-floor and bumped on the garden underneath as Sebastian watched it, in utter disbelief.

"Damn," said Pat.

"Shhh..." Sebastian warned her.

Laura said nothing as she watched, rigid with fear. Quentin came down the stairs from the terrace. He was smiling triumphantly.

"How close did it land?" asked Sebastian.

The antidote had landed near the north-east boundary of the terrace, perfectly adjacent to the shed which had the zombie perched on it.

To get to the package, one would have to climb the single flight of stairs to the terrace, open the door, walk around the structure that housed the staircase, either clockwise or counter clockwise, go out to the north-east corner, retrieve the package and come back.

"What do we do now?" asked Pat.

"We wait till it's dark," Quentin replied.

The law and order situation was gradually deteriorating. The farther they moved from the zombies, Matt noticed, the worse it got.

Despite the army and the police, the announcement regarding the sealing-off of the Americas for an undetermined duration of time was not being taken well.

People had been told to stay inside their homes. The museum on 63rd street, among others, had been converted into a shelter for the homeless. But now that they had been inoculated and the zombies would be long dead before they reached far north, people had taken to the streets, demonstrating. These were testing times. Rough and morose.

Bart Romney was in touch with Hung Ti, the Japanese Premier who was a shrewd businessman and Romney's boss.

Bart worked at New York University (NYU) as an assistant professor, but was in fact a Japanese spy. He usually reported back to Japan on the progress of the microbiology lab at NYU. He had been contacted by the Japanese secret service a few years ago when Japan and USA were co-anchoring a research project to cure mental depression.

It appeared that depression wasn't a genetic disorder; it was the human response to external stimuli. This was the theoretical ground for the project to be undertaken by both Japan and America together, or to be precise, by NYU and the Japanese Premier.

They proposed that the degree to which human beings respond

to the world around them determined their state of mind. These seemingly unconnected variables gave rise to a wealth of correlations and excitement.

They applied their research and were again proven right. The more a person responded to his or her circumstances, the happier that person was. Depression was defined as people's inability to react to people, things and events. All that was needed was a way to take away people's inability to react and get them closer to the world, make them experience people and instances more fully.

The microbiology team, among others, had been informed of this project internally and it was Bart who had come up with a solution.

A virus that would encourage people to react. A bug.

It would cling to the host's neurons and allow electric synapses to pass more efficiently.

In theory, everyone was excited and Hung Ti himself had contacted Bart and added him on the payroll.

The result was a secret test which was carried out in the city of Stillwater Oklahoma where a rat mutated the virus. This is where things went wrong and the virus reacted in a manner which was contrary to its objective.

It rendered a person completely ineffective and unable to react with his or her surroundings unless to spread the handicap further. This was the conclusive and final stage of depression.

Bart was liked by the academic community but he also had political aspirations. Both Hung Ti and he had already had several discussions as to how the situation could be leveraged in the best possible manner.

The virus had worked, no doubt about it. Only if the mutation could be controlled, well, then they were home.

They had decided that rather than doing nothing, Bart would take a pro-evacuation stand and champion the cause of lifting the quarantine. Once the United States had been gassed, that is.

And his first task was to hold a demonstration in front of NYU.

Matt was watching him on the news channel. He was inside the big airport hangar where the evacuees had been temporarily set up. There was a dark patch on the hangar floor, just where Matt and his family had been stationed.

The patch was a probably result of an oil spilled in the past. Matt found himself staring at it for hours.

Radha and he were chosen for a random bunch of experiments in the hope of discovering a drug which could make humans immune against the zombie bug.

He had been injected with the drug the same morning he had landed.

Now, he found, that try as he may, he didn't have to look around to kill the hopeless hours which would normally have hung around his head, unwilling to pass. He could contently stare at one spot, unaware of the hours that passed him by.

Even as he looked at the patch on the ground, Hillary and Bridget were arguing about something. Matt snapped out of his trance.

Once the city was gassed, the evacuees would be given accommodation in the city itself.

A lot of people had fled to the Bahamas before a complete quarantine had been imposed, following the stray crash which had taken place north of Monterrey.

Their empty houses would now be assigned to the people who had come from the south. They had been told that they would not be able to return because of some big government project which was being run back in Oklahoma.

Matt turned his gaze back from the television to the small, dark spot.

Sebastian looked at his watch.

11:15 p.m., Friday, 4 August.

He was handsome, a little too handsome for his 85 kilo frame. He had coal black eyes and eyebrows to match and a pleasing angular face. Women flocked around him and he fended them off.

The thing about Sebastian was that he was prone to fall in love. Ever so often, and that sort of precluded his being in any one relationship.

While at his age, women wanted more than sex and love. They wanted security, some wanted children.

Sebastian thought about the last girl he had loved – Tina.

He wondered about the last thing he had said to her.

Did it fully reflect the weight of his emotions?

Should he have said something else?

Even as Sebastian was trying to force his emotions upon Tina, sparing little thought for her predicament, he saw that the family had assembled around him in the living room.

They were continuing where they had left off. Which was how they were going to get the antidote back in time.

And, just like the last time, nobody was saying anything.

Sebastian cleared his mind of Tina and tried to snap back to the present.

The way he saw it, there was only two choices.

Either they crept outside and got close enough to the zombie to shoot it, and kill it, or they could try snatching the packet from under its very eyes.

The second route felt considerably more risky, but the first route required a confrontation.

"The way I see it," began Sebastian, "we have two choices." He paused. Nobody said anything.

"We can either shoot the zombie and then retrieve the package."

Laura made to say something. Then she thought the better of it.

"Or we can try sneaking the package in," continued Sebastian. "During which, if we attract the zombie's attention, we will have to shoot a moving target."

He let his words hang in the air. Since the life of each family member was at stake, the decision had to be made by all of them, preferably unanimously.

Sebastian suggested a vote.

Quentin cleared his throat. "I think the second option is more feasible," he said.

"I say we shoot the bastard and be done with it," said Sebastian.

"And I say," said Pat firmly, "that we take the quieter option."

Sebastian looked at Pat as if to argue when Laura said, "I vote we sneak the package in."

And so it was decided. Democratically.

The family had not spoken a word about who would get the package.

Sebastian managed a metaphorical shrug and announced that it would be him who would be retrieving the package while Quentin would keep watch.

Quentin agreed.

All that remained was for everyone to grab their guns and decide who would stand where while Sebastian and Quentin went up to the terrace.

Sebastian walked up the stairs and a terrible thought struck him as he saw Pat grip the stock of her shotgun meaningfully.

If he was bitten while getting the package, it would be Pat who would be waiting for him.

The moon was fuller now and the terrace was bathed in its light.

Sebastian checked his weapon; the silver Smith and Wesson, the one he had practiced on. It was loaded. The safety was off. Now, it was time.

Quentin kept a black Smith and Wesson in his pocket and carried the shotgun in his hands, with the barrel pointing downwards.

Silently, they climbed up the stairs to the terrace.

Sebastian's stomach lurched inside.

'What if I get bitten?' he thought, again.

He pushed the thought away from his mind as he reached the landing.

The landing was covered in a glass box with a 360 degree view of the terrace and had a door which faced west and towards the driveway

Cautiously, Sebastian crouched low on the landing and waited for Quentin.

Quentin came and crouched beside him.

Slowly, with infinite caution, Sebastian raised his head and turned towards the TT shed.

He had to stand up to see it.

His mind noticed two horrifying things simultaneously.

The first was the zombie itself.

The zombie was a teenager, complete in training shoes and a T-shirt. Must have been at a mall when all this happened.

The face of the zombie was unrecognizable as a teenager, though. It had the eyes of an animal, yellow and watchful. There were streaks of mud and blood clotting its face and some of the skin had been bitten off.

Didn't a zombie feel pain, Sebastian wondered.

But the really terrible part was that the zombie had now moved.

It had been crouched on the north-west corner of the shed, the part which faced the courtyard and the driveway.

Now it had moved along the north boundary and positioned itself on the north-east corner, which overlooked the part of the terrace where the package lay.

There was no way to get the package without being seen. Option 2 was kaput.

Sebastian ducked back down again. Quentin was on the floor.

"It's directly above the package and looking at it," whispered Sebastian.

"We'll have to wait," whispered Quentin.

Sebastian closed his eyes. He thought he was going to be sick. All the tension, the adrenaline, the fear; and now they would have to wait.

No, he decided, it was now or never.

He nodded to Quentin to stand guard. They both stood up slowly.

The door was made of toughened glass in a strong plastic frame. Which meant it was virtually soundproof.

Sebastian lifted the handle and turned the knob around. Now the door was unlocked.

The zombie still sat watching the package.

Sebastian moved forward to open the door.

Quentin, who was standing beside him, placed a hand on his shoulder.

Sebastian shrugged it off, gently.

He bent double, opened the door and crept on to the terrace.

Without the protection of toughened glass or brick and concrete, Sebastian felt alarm bells going off in his head.

All it would take for the zombie was to turn its head an inch and the attack was inevitable.

To take another step now would only be increasing the chances that the zombie would reach him before he could get back inside the glass landing.

In front of him, a few paces away, facing the door was the west wall of the terrace, overlooking the driveway.

To his right was the TT shed.

A few strides and he was pressed against the south side of the shed.

Quentin crept after Sebastian and gently closed the door behind them.

He crouched low and trained his shotgun on the zombie.

Neither of them made a sound.

Sebastian waited for a minute. The zombie seemed unaware of the presence of the two intruders on the terrace.

Sebastian transferred the pistol to his right hand. This was the tricky part. If the zombie sensed their presence on the terrace, they would have no choice but to shoot it.

Sebastian had seen how the zombies moved. Fast and fearless. He didn't want to try his luck with the gun. This meant he had to do this with absolute silence and stealth.

With infinite patience, he slid his right foot out by a few millimetres. He balanced himself with his gun as he brought the left foot to match with his first step.

He was moving along the south wall of the TT shed. The roof extended over the boundaries of the shed, to provide shade to anyone who stood or sat next to the wall of the shed.

It also provided Sebastian shelter from the zombie's ever alert eyes.

Sebastian had almost made it to the corner without making a sound.

Turning the corner, however, was more difficult because once he did, he would be on the same side of the shed where the zombie sat and kept watch.

Seeing from the corner of the eye was more effective than staring straight at a thing.

If the zombie sensed any movement, Sebastian would have to face the repercussions. Undoubtedly. And run back, empty-handed.

Just as he reached the south-east corner of the shed, Sebastian turned towards Quentin for confirmation that the zombie was still in the same position.

Quentin didn't move a muscle. His arms were taut and the gun was aimed at the zombie.

He wasn't even looking at Sebastian.

Slowly, with infinite caution, Sebastian turned around the corner.

The zombie was quiet, which meant it had sensed nothing. Sebastian smelt shit and blood. And the smell of something dying. Decaying.

The zombie's body was technically not dead, but slowly dying without proper medical attention and the care that it needed. Its wounds were gangrenous and filled with maggots. Its clothes tattered and spent. Only its eyes were alert and filled with a strange yellowish light.

Like a wolf. Or a reptile. A very intelligent reptile.

Now the package was in Sebastian's line of sight.

White and innocuous, it lay among the other packages that the passing planes had showered. It was just a few metres away.

It would all have been so simple, but for the solitary zombie.

The seconds now stretched taut. Sebastian was covered in sweat. He wasn't sure he would be able to run when the time came. Perhaps he had bitten off more than he could chew.

Again, Sebastian began the painstaking process of pressing his body against the glass pane of the shed and moving forward, one millimetre at a time.

He realised that he was sweating profusely.

Fortunately, the zombie would never smell him. But the foul stench of the zombie was more unbearable than ever.

Sebastian took small shallow breaths as he moved.

In the stillness of the night, broken only by zombie screeches, Sebastian could hear his steps creak.

He cursed silently and pushed himself on every step. One more, he promised himself. One more and I'll stop. Turn around and go back.

Now he was standing directly underneath the place where the zombie sat; the north-east corner of the shed.

The package was a few paces ahead of him.

Both zombie and Sebastian were looking at the same package.

'Was it really watching the package?' thought Sebastian. 'Were they intelligent?'

Sebastian had no idea if the zombie had moved. He could no longer see Quentin.

This had been a bad idea. They should have waited. Perhaps they should have tried shooting the zombie first and then retrieved the package.

Trying to outrun the zombie would be difficult. Especially if the zombie had already moved along the shed.

Then it would be directly between the door to the terrace and him. Sebastian's hands were sweating so much he was afraid the gun would slip out.

And in that moment when action was imperative, his brain was flashed with a childhood memory.

It was about a simple game he used to play with his cousins.

There were two teams. Both teams had their safety enclosures on opposite sides of a garden.

In the centre, there was a circle and in the centre of the circle lay a handkerchief. A whistle would blow and both teams would send one team member out of the enclosure. The two contestants from each team would then walk along the circle.

The objective was to grab the handkerchief and then make it back to the respective safety enclosure without coming in contact with the other contestant who would chase the one who had the handkerchief.

The dog and the bone, the game was called, remembered Sebastian.

Only one person could walk away with the bone.

Sebastian wondered idly whether it would be the zombie or him who would win this chase.

He transferred his gun to his left hand, ever so slowly.

Then he got ready.

He checked his balance, closed his eyes and opened them.

Nothing happened. Nothing would, till *he* started it. This thought gave Sebastian a little confidence.

It was time. He forgot about everything else, focused on the package, pushed himself off the wall of the shed and darted out.

The warm air hit his sweat-soaked chest like a cool wind. He made it two steps towards the package when he felt a rush of air above him.

Sebastian had been fast. The zombie had been faster. It had reacted almost instantaneously and leapt off the shed.

It just hadn't been fast enough.

It had landed a few inches behind Sebastian with a loud thump.

Sebastian reached the package without turning around. His mind was now racing in survival mode.

As he grabbed the package, he felt a sick sensation in his stomach.

The zombie was back on its feet and was looking at Sebastian. It let out a loud screech.

Sebastian didn't pause as he picked up the package and ran towards the glass landing to his right.

There was a loud gunshot. Almost deafening.

Sebastian ignored the ringing in his ears as he started towards the glass landing, wishing with all his heart that Quentin had at least winged the bastard.

But it was not to be.

The zombie came at Sebastian diagonally, trying to come between Sebastian and the glass landing.

Sebastian immediately turned track and ran instead towards the south wall of the terrace and away from the zombie.

The zombie also turned and followed Sebastian.

Sebastian now ran south-west and away from the glass landing. The zombie was inches behind him.

Then Sebastian, who had played plenty of basketball in his youth, ducked left and moved right.

The zombie's hand grazed him and its knee caught him on the thigh as the zombie stumbled and fell against the east wall of the terrace.

Had the wall been the height of a regular wall, the zombie would have gone over.

But Matt had constructed his apartment on this level. So the zombie hit its head against the wall of Matt's apartment and bounced back, dazed.

Pain flooded through Sebastian's leg which he ignored as he straightened and ran towards the glass landing and safety.

That he could have shot the zombie had not even occurred to Sebastian. Not that it mattered. The gun was in Sebastian's left hand, attached as if surgically and Sebastian had been terrible with his left hand when he had practiced.

The glass landing was now in front of him. All he needed to do was turn a corner and enter the door facing west. Quentin, who was now in sight, standing inside the glass enclosure was holding the door open.

Fortunately, the door opened inwards, and would allow Quentin to close it safely.

Sebastian's heart was in his mouth as he rounded the first corner. He could hear the zombie's wild rasping breath, the sound of his own heartbeat as he turned and felt the zombie's hand miss him by inches.

He gathered his balance and dashed into the doorway while Quentin closed the door shut and locked it.

The zombie threw itself at the door.

The door shook, but held.

The zombie screeched and roared.

Sebastian looked down at his hands.

In one hand, he held the Smith and Wesson; in the other hand, he was holding the white package.

His hands were trembling. But it was done.

Quentin took a step back from the door as the zombie hurled itself again.

"They are climbing up the tree," shouted Pat from the drawing room.

And then Sebastian heard a loud shotgun blast. It came from the kitchen.

He stood up and ran down the stairs. Quentin was still standing in front of the terrace door, as the zombie snarled and threw itself against the door.

"Quick," Pat shouted as Sebastian passed her. She still had the shotgun in her hand.

Sebastian, though terrified, was still thinking clearly.

He was terrified because he had realised that if enough zombies made it up the tree, they would certainly break down the terrace door.

He wondered if Quentin had realised the same thing.

He wanted to shout at the top of his lungs and tell Quentin the danger they were in. But fear took away his voice. It settled somewhere in his throat and refused to leave.

He put his pistol in his pocket and picked up a shotgun from the dining table.

He heard another gunshot form the kitchen.

The tree could be seen both from his parents' bedroom and the kitchen. But the bedroom window was accessible from the tree. The widows were huge and occupied the top half of one side of the room.

A zombie could easily jump in if they were opened.

The kitchen was the only place they could pick off the zombies as they tried to climb the tree.

Sebastian turned around the corner and skidded into the kitchen.

The first thing he heard was a shrill screeching noise which hit him like a dull ache. Laura was standing at the far end of the kitchen, next to the window.

The window was open and she was leaning out, her shotgun

pointing towards the tree.

'Bang,' it thundered.

The sound in the enclosed space was deafening.

"Now!" she shouted, flecks of spittle flying from her mouth. Her short hair flew wild as she discharged the sixth shot into the tree.

Sebastian took up position beside her and pointed his own gun at the tree.

The tree was only a few metres away and the chances of missing the zombies, zero.

A zombie, an old woman in a long dress, had made it to the top branches and was climbing over the TT shed.

The angle was too acute for Sebastian to get a shot from his shotgun. Instead, he aimed at a zombie directly in front of him. The boy was no older than 18. He had red hair and blue eyes. The wide eyes now had a terrible expression, that of violence, of victory and of death.

Amid the loud and deafening roar of the gun, the shoulder numbing recoil, Sebastian saw the blood squirt out of the zombies' chest as the shotgun shells perforated it.

The zombie fell from the tree, finally at peace.

As Sebastian watched in horror, another zombie clambered over the tree onto the shed.

"Shoot the branches," shouted Sebastian though he could hardly hear his own voice.

Laura's barrage had already clipped most of the branches at eye level.

Sebastian saw two more zombies about to clamber on to the shed at the top of the terrace.

He ignored them and shot at the branches which were at his eye level.

Calmly and coolly, he pumped his remaining five shots into the tree, indifferent to the presence of the zombies that climbed the tree.

The screeching, howling, the baying for blood, and the occasional shotgun blast were followed by a zombie exploding into a pool of blood.

"Again," he shouted.

Laura was having trouble reloading her gun.

Pat who had picked up the remaining shotgun, pushed Laura roughly out of the way.

"Shoot the branches," Sebastian shouted.

Pat nodded and discharged her shots into the tree.

"You're aiming too high," Sebastian shouted between the shots.

He had no idea if Pat could hear him.

"Quentin!" Laura roared. She had given up trying to reload and had gone back into the drawing room.

A second later, Quentin charged into the kitchen with his shotgun.

He pushed both Sebastian and Pat aside and pumped his quota of rounds into the tree.

Sebastian, who had managed to load his shotgun took his turn and in quick succession, discharged six shots, systematically into the branches.

Pat had reloaded her gun and followed him.

And then, they all stopped.

The silence but for the screeches was almost welcome.

They examined their handiwork.

The tree had been cut in half by the unending deluge of shotgun shells. A few thin but leafy branches still extended up beyond the first floor, but only a cat could climb them.

"They are on the terrace," shouted Laura from the drawing room.

Sebastian, Quentin and Pat ran towards drawing room, the three of them holding their weapons like prized possessions.

Laura was standing at the foot of the stairs, which led to the terrace. Her shotgun was aimed at the terrace door.

There was a single flight of stairs facing south. The door was to the west. The zombies, after breaking down the door, would only have to turn to their left to access the staircase.

Sebastian hoped that Laura's gun was loaded.

He ran past her and halfway up the stairs.

There were around ten zombies putting their combined weight on the glass door.

The glass was toughened, but the lock wasn't. It would snap and break. It was only a matter of time. Time, Sebastian calculated, was something they certainly did not have.

The zombies had mustered opposite the terrace door. There was ample room for all eleven zombies that had climbed upon the terrace.

They were pushing and grunting, in unison.

The frame of the door rattled as it was pushed inwards.

The Parkers had assembled around the foot of the stairs, each one holding a fully loaded shotgun.

In front of the doorway to Sebastian's parents' room, stood Sebastian and Quentin, side by side.

The doorway was a few steps away from where the stairs ended. This meant both Sebastian and Quentin would be right in the middle of the attack.

To Sebastian's right stood Laura, perpendicular to the foot of the stairs. She would shoot the horde from one side as they descended.

Pat stationed herself next to the dining table at the east end of the drawing room. It would be her job to shoot the stray zombies which the others might miss.

Sebastian took a deep breath and looked at Quentin's hands. They were trembling. He noticed that his own hands were trembling too.

The zombies outside the drawing room had amplified their squealing, as if they were anticipating the kill.

There wasn't enough peace to think. Nor did they have any time to waste.

The terrace door groaned for one last time before it came crashing.

Three zombies fell through the open doorway but were immediately trampled. The rest of them rushed in and hit the toughened glass at the other end of the door.

The zombies that came after them, turned towards their left and saw the Parkers.

Their desperation had now turned into frenzy.

With traces of blood, gut and faeces in their hair, faces and clothes, they screeched and ran down the stairs as one.

The shotgun in Sebastian's hand thundered.

He hit the first zombie in the chest. A deranged looking woman of around forty.

The zombie flew back under the full impact of the pellets and its body crumpled against the stairs.

The one next to it suffered the same fate as Quentin's shotgun also came to life. Quentin had timed his shot well.

The plump man of forty, who had been rushing down the stairs, in a mass of teeth and blood stopped dead in his tracks as his head was blown off.

Sebastian had no time to take aim again and fired into the mass of zombies leaping down the stairs.

He hit one which had reached the bottom of the stairs and was about to pounce on him. The shot had hit the zombie's shoulder and passed into the zombie behind him.

The zombie with the injured shoulder fell back before it charged again.

Dispassionately, carefully, Sebastian timed his next shot better and shot it through the chest.

Laura and Pat were shooting indiscriminately into the mess of writhing bodies pouring down the stairs.

Quentin was taking care of the front.

Sebastian took the time he had, to aim at the target.

Two zombies came down on his side one after another.

Sebastian made the mistake of aiming at the one who was second in that order. It had been an easy shot and Sebastian had taken it without much thought.

The one in lead landed at the foot of the stairs and rolled to its left, towards Laura.

The zombie, a rather large beefy man with large beefy hands, a farmer by his build and appearance, was now on the floor directly between Sebastian and Laura.

It sat up in a crouch and looked at Laura. Then it screeched.

Laura would have been less than human had she not taken the shot.

Sebastian turned his gaze to his right and saw his mother aiming her shotgun in his direction.

He opened his mouth to shout 'no', but got no further.

The zombie started to spring at Laura and she fired downwards at the zombie's head.

Sebastian's world exploded in colour as the shotgun pellets ricochetted off the floor and scattered inside the drawing room.

He sensed that he was falling and that the ground was rushing up to meet him.

Then he lost consciousness.

He was lying on the floor when he opened his eyes.

To his left, Quentin stood still, the shotgun in his hand pointed at the stairs. But the gun wasn't firing.

Quentin's right arm and shoulder were drenched in blood.

Sebastian watched as the gun slipped from Quentin's lifeless fingers and fell with a clatter. And then Quentin, with his chest shredded by pellets, dropped dead like a sack of potatoes.

He saw Pat being overpowered by two zombies. She was screaming like a helpless pig as one of them grabbed her neck.

One more zombie had survived and was pounding on the door to Sebastian's room, behind which Laura was hiding.

Sebastian tried moving his head but passed out because of excruciating pain.

Sebastian could smell them.

Mixed with the scent of gunpowder in the air was the familiar decaying smell. Their smell.

He opened his eyes, slowly, not knowing which part of him had fallen off. At least he was still alive and human.

Pat was a few meters away from him, pounding at the door to his room behind which Laura had taken shelter.

She was accompanied by three other zombies.

They were now screeching and howling for Laura.

Sebastian couldn't imagine what Laura was going through at the moment. But he had his own troubles to focus on.

He didn't move his head this time. Slowly he swivelled his eyes to look at himself. His right leg had been shredded by the passing pellets and was bleeding profusely. Surprisingly, he didn't feel anything.

His shotgun was lying a few feet to his left, next to Quentin's cold dead body.

He couldn't get them all, he thought. Not from his position on the floor. And if he tried, they would come charging at him instead.

His eyes caught the sight of the clock on the far side of the wall.

It was 12:10 a.m.

Less than an hour has passed since Parkers were sitting in the same drawing room, discussing the best course of action. The thought filled Sebastian with pain.

Very quietly, softly, Sebastian moved his right leg. A wave of intense pain streaked up his nerves. He clenched his teeth to curb the pain, his eyes wet with tears. He let his leg lie still.

The zombies were pushing hard now.

'There is still plenty of time to get the antidote,' thought Sebastian.

But the antidote wasn't the problem now.

Sebastian needed to get further from his bedroom door before he started shooting at the zombies who were trying to break it down.

He tried to shift his weight to his left. Perhaps he could roll towards the dining table. But the pain threatened to make him pass out again.

He had lined up his shotgun on the zombies and considered his options. The package lay on the dining table, right where he had left it.

Sebastian made another attempt. This time, he pulled himself a little towards the dining table. It worked. The pain was lesser this time.

The door of his room was not as strong as the two front doors. The lock splintered and the door crashed open.

Sebastian turned and shot without thinking. And he shot again.

Two zombies died, their backs shredded to confetti. One of them was Pat.

The remaining two dithered for a millisecond at the edge of doorway, confused as to which way they should turn, then rushed inside the room.

From inside the room, Sebastian heard another shot in reply.

Laura had put one down. Which meant one more was left.

He dragged his pistol out. His shotgun was left with one shot. He had no time to reload.

There were no more shots from inside the room.

Sebastian pointed his gun at the open doorway and waited. His mother came first. Screeching and fast.

Sebastian shot her in the chest thrice before the other zombie ran from behind her falling body.

Sebastian emptied his magazine into it.

He kept pressing the trigger long after that, the clicking noise echoing in the empty hall. Then he was alone.

Sebastian put the gun aside and dragged himself towards the dining table. He gripped the corner with one hand and pulled himself up. With one last ounce of remaining energy he flung himself into a chair.

The moonlight shone down bright through the overhead skylight on the white package. He had sacrificed everything to get it. His family, his life, perhaps even his ability to walk. And if the pain in his head was any indication, even a grey cell or two.

His watch showed 12:37 a.m.

He opened the package carefully.

As promised, there were four ampoules preloaded in syringes. Along with two tourniquets and a book of directions.

He tied one tourniquet around his leg to stop the bleeding and the other around his arm.

He flicked his arm to expose a vein.

Then, carefully, he picked up one of the syringes and brought it close to his arm. He picked a vein and without another thought plunged the needle in and pressed the trigger.

The he lay back and closed his eyes.

It was 4:45 a.m. when he woke up.

He was dizzy from the loss of blood and in urgent need of medication.

But in the streaking light of dawn, he witnessed something strange.

From his position at the dining table, he could see outside the west facing windows of the drawing room.

He heard it before he saw it. The sound of a chopper.

It landed on the roof of their neighbour's house. Some soldiers came out. Then they got busy with something which Sebastian couldn't see because the chopper was blocking his view.

Fifteen minutes later, the men climbed back into the chopper and took off.

De Gaulle's cure, the virus was called. America had been gassed twice already.

The US government was not at all interested in finding out the origin of the outbreak which had taken the life of millions, and while more lives were still at stake. But what was widely discussed in conversations was the invention of the antidote that had saved the world.

Now after careful inoculation, America would be gassed again, this time with another deadly virus.

But first they would send in 'The Security Detail' which was hailed as one of the bravest, if not the largest military manoeuvre the world had ever seen. It was made up of volunteers, men and women. People who were aware that once they entered the United States of America, they wouldn't be able to leave for the foreseeable future.

Some brought their near and dear ones along with them. Some left them behind, choosing their safety over their company.

Rocky woke up and brushed his teeth. He was neither married nor committed in any way. Neither was he inclined towards any humanitarian causes. He was a mercenary for hire. And the cost of going to a country, which had been indefinitely quarantined, no matter how developed, was very, very high.

He could leave America a rich man. Or he could stay.

He had been promised a house in Kansas. The house was bought cheap from the previous owner who had evacuated the country.

In the eyes of the public, he was just one of the members of

The Security Detail, easily identifiable by their blue and grey uniforms. An Indian who had volunteered to save the world from any threat, external or of its own making.

But the real mission was far more dangerous.

Rocky ran a hand through his dark hair. He was handsome at 42; a delicate jaw, high cheekbones and wonderful laughing eyes. Also, a stone-cold killer.

The enemy, from what he had been told, wasn't human. Not this time. He smiled to himself. The enemy, he knew, was always human.

It was 6 August. By early morning the next day, he would be flown into America. He would soon be a part of three hundred other mercenaries in the employ of Hung Ti, mixed with regular soldiers.

The Security Detail members were assigned different roles in different parts of the country.

Rocky's identification papers read, 'special forces'. Hung Ti's team had even worked on his background. His records showed that he had done tours of duty in Iraq, North Korea and some in ISIS territory. This was true indeed. But the records neglected to mention which side he had been fighting for.

Not many people knew much about Rocky or who he had been working for. He had been to Oklahoma once before, only briefly, to observe a target at a farmer's festival. He wondered what he would see there now. He awaited the new challenge and was curious to know what future had in store for him. He was lost in these thoughts as he sat inside the military transport plane and nodded at a pretty woman.

The last six months had been spent idle and for a man who counted on a high dose of adrenaline for a healthy, daily existence, it had been a lifetime.

He smiled inwardly as the first bits of Oklahoma arrived under their plane.

It had been four days since the incident, and the military takeover of Oklahoma was complete.

The wounded and dying, and the ones who were now being rehabilitated in military hospitals were the only ones that remained. Mostly everybody else had taken the deal the government had offered and had moved out of Oklahoma.

Rocky's contact in America was a certain Bart Romney. Rocky was to follow his instructions to the letter.

Yes, the task was dangerous, and Rocky would be well rewarded for doing it.

The Commander of the air base to which Matt had been evacuated to with his family, had called him for an interview. It was related to the chemical tests that were being performed on Radha and him.

"How far has the research on the cure progressed?" Matt asked while sitting in front of the Commander.

The Commander was a short, balding man with a bushy moustache. He was well past middle age. He had a halting way of speaking, as if he was trying to stress every syllable. Might have been a consequence of his long years of giving (and taking) precise orders while serving in the army.

Matt gave him a haughty stare. Despite the grim situation, this special treatment from the military made him feel confident.

The Commander's office was at the military base. It was twenty kilometres further from Matt's new apartment located on the bank of river Hudson. The apartment was allocated to Matt by the New American military.

Matt had been picked up in a Humvee today, by a personal escort along with the driver. The escort had smiled politely all along the journey, but chose not to answer any of Matt's questions.

Matt had many questions like why was he, Matt selected for the tests. Or what did they want from him now. Probably, the escort didn't know, Matt thought.

"We already have the cure," replied the Commander, a little hesitantly.

"You mean, I am immune to the zombie virus? The tests worked."

The Commander pushed the table with one hand and swivelled his chair. The fact that his feet didn't touch the ground was of little consequence to him.

"Well, yes," he replied at length.

"Great. That means you can lift the quarantine," continued Matt.

"As soon as we're 100% sure," replied the Commander with a polite smile. "I am told that some tests are still left. Which is why I asked to see you," he said steeping his fingers on the table

Matt waited while the Commander examined his own fingernails.

"You have been asked to return to Stillwater," he finally said.

"What?" blurted out Matt.

"Only for a few days since that's where the project headquarters are," the commander now leaned back in his chair as if the deal was done. "We need you to go there because there is certain equipment that can't be carted over here. New tests, you see."

The commander smiled cheerfully.

Matt wondered how Hillary would react. It had been a month since they had shifted to their new house and Radha was vulnerable to change. Matt's absence for a few days would certainly qualify for a big change.

He was still deciding how to break the news to Hillary as he walked into his apartment on the fifth floor.

"What did he want?" Bridget asked as she came out of the kitchen.

Matt did not want to respond to the same question twice. "Where is Hillary?" he asked.

Bridget felt insulted.

"She's taken Radha out for a walk," she replied. "Phillip went along. I stayed back to mind the house. Was it something serious?" she persisted.

"No. But I have to go to Stillwater for some tests," said Matt.

Bridget clamped her hands to her mouth. She had always been the one for theatrics.

"To that zombie-infested pit?" she said.

Matt sighed.

He mumbled something inaudible and then turned away from Bridget.

He settled down on the couch in the living room and turned on the TV.

The government was taking good care of them. They had been given this house, daily rations, and the promise of a working society once the quarantine was lifted. Which would be any day now, thought Matt.

Bridget went and sat beside Matt.

"Isn't there something you were doing in the kitchen?" Matt asked rudely.

Bridget didn't answer. She just sniffed and then sat with her arms crossed, her mouth in a pout.

Matt mindlessly flipped through TV channels while Bridget made disapproving noises in the background.

The door opened and Phillip entered with his hands full of groceries.

"The government is taking good care of us," he said cheerfully from the door as he saw Matt sitting with Bridget in front of the television.

"That's exactly what I was saying," replied Matt switching off the TV.

Radha entered next and screamed with delight as she saw Matt. She ran at him, her arms outstretched.

Matt got up and lifted her up in the air. Then he brought her near his face and held her tight.

"Feel Daddy's beard," he told her.

She began stroking his cheek.

"It's still the same size since I left you. Was I really gone that long?"

Radha chuckled with joy and pretended to punch Matt.

Matt gently put Radha on the floor as Hillary entered and smiled at the sight.

"He's going to Stillwater," rang out Bridget's voice. She was talking to Phillip in the kitchen while he was unloading the groceries. "Is he crazy?" Bridget continued.

Matt groaned inwardly. Had Bridget forgotten that she was not in her large Stillwater apartment? Or was this just her way of getting back at him for ignoring her?

"Who's going to Stillwater?" asked Hillary as she led Radha to the bathroom by her hand. She sounded anxious.

Bridget poked her head out of the kitchen. "Matt," she said.

Hillary who was now making sure that Radha washed her hands, stopped dead.

She came out of the bathroom. "Really?" she asked looking at Matt. "Was that what the meeting was about?"

"Ah, yes," replied Matt. "They want to me finish the tests. They claim to have already found the cure."

"What about Radha? They don't want her to go?"

"No, I guess not," replied Matt. He should have asked the Commander that. But he was so excited about visiting his hometown, perhaps even go see his home, that it hadn't occurred to him. In a way, he was glad that he did not. Matt didn't want to risk Radha's life by reminding the Commander of her and making her accompany him to that zombie-infested pit, as Bridget had called it.

"Where is Daddy going?" asked Radha as she came out of the bathroom.

"Honey," replied Matt quickly and reassuringly, "remember those tests the military did on us?"

Radha stood at the doorway and nodded.

"Well, they called Daddy to Stillwater to do some more tests."

For some inexplicable reason, Radha started crying inconsolably. Neither Matt nor Hillary could understand why the news had affected her so badly.

Bridget looked at Radha with a worried frown on her face. The rosary between her fingers was moving in fast rotations now. She was feeling the same as Radha, it seemed, sans the tears though and pronounced this as an ill omen.

"Why can't you say no?" she asked for the umpteenth time.

"The virus binds perfectly with the cells in this man's body." Said Dr. Riwazzo, who was dressed in a dark suit under his lab coat.

Dr. Riwazzo was one of the leading immune-virologists of the country. He was determined not to leave any stone unturned. After all, the success of his research required funding by the most powerful and discreet businessmen from all over the world.

Being discrete was essential. As was being well dressed.

"Once this virus, the 'evolution virus' as it is called, attaches itself to the brain's neurons, it fights the zombie virus and doesn't let it take hold."

He was standing in front of two large screens of the operation theatre. The operation theatre had a viewing gallery where the businessmen were seated. His eyes gleamed with a hint of victory while he explained the nature of the virus to the many legible suitors of his research. Riwazzo was sure that he would convince one of the astute men in business present and get whatever support his research needed.

"But gentlemen," said Dr. Riwazzo, "This is more than a cure! What we are seeing is evolution."

The group didn't react.

"Have you ever wondered why you feel depressed?" asked Dr. Riwazzo, a little disappointed at their wooden faces, so unimpressed by his presentation.

"It is the inability to react to things," continued Riwazzo. "The evolution virus removes this inability. Imagine being able to cooperate with the world, to unite with the universe seamlessly."

The other side of the table was suddenly full of surprised and uncertain whispers. Riwazzo's idea was surreal and had reflections of a possible future. The fact that they would be the harbingers of America's future had filled the businessmen with sudden excitement and pride.

"The earliest form of the evolution virus didn't work. As some of you know, the virus mutated in a rat and created what is now known to you as the zombie bug," continued Dr. Riwazzo. He now had the complete attention of the audience.

A hushed silence followed Riwazzo's revelation.

"We have harnessed this mutated virus and further mutated it, this time in the right direction," he added.

"The zombie virus completely cuts off the person from external stimulus," and Dr. Riwazzo paused as the doors of the operation theatre flung opened.

The audience gasped. Some of them even stood up as a conscious zombie was wheeled into the operation theatre. It was strapped to a vertical gurney. While roving its pale eyes across the room, it often paused to stare at the faces of the nervous human beings who shuddered even at the thought of being in the same room with a zombie.

"One can see the effects immediately," continued Dr. Riwazzo gesturing at the zombie.

The zombie screeched and snarled. Then it cowered as it saw it was outnumbered.

"Counter intuitively, the evolution virus helps you regain focus and stay calm, despite opening you up to absorb more of the world around you."

Dr. Riwazzo walked up to the zombie. He continued talking as he moved.

"This is Z129," he said.

Then without any intimation, he plunged a needle straight into the zombie's spinal cord.

He withdrew some spinal fluid and nodded at the assistant who started wheeling the zombie back.

The audience seemed disappointed. Half of them were more interested in the zombie than the experiment.

"These cells signify raw evolution," said Dr. Riwazzo, gesturing with the needle, lifting it high in the air to underline what he just said.

The audience seemed captivated now.

"But at the other end of the spectrum is what I have named the 'evolution virus'. These cells will now be treated so that when they attach to the neurons of their host, they will do the exact opposite of what they did to Z129," he said, rising the fluid-filled needle once again.

He put the syringe on a table and crossed his arms, waiting.

"What does this evolution feel like?" one of the audience members, a man in a business suit, shot the question in Riwazzo's direction.

The businessman's hands were stretched in front of him in excitement as he asked the question.

"The drug makes your mind expand beyond limit," replied Dr. Riwazzo. "Don't think of it as an experience, but as a means to the future. A broad and open mind paves the way to endless opportunities waiting to be explored. The things which human beings could never have imagined."

The man in the business suit sat down with a wide smile. Riwazzo's answer had pleased him immensely.

After the demonstration was over, a man called Ray Burburry came to the operation theatre when Dr. Riwazzo was cleaning up.

"I want to try it, purely for business purposes. Actually, I have a new business model in mind," he said without preamble, sinking his hands inside the deep pockets on either side of his grey-black trousers.

Dr. Riwazzo stared at him in utter disbelief.

"You don't know who I am? Allow me to introduce myself properly. My name is Ray Burburry, the most successful pharmaceutical businessman around."

Riwazzo found his hand being taken forward and shaken forcefully.

"Listen, we can make billions with this idea, literally," promised Burburry gesturing towards the syringe which still perched atop one of the wooden tables inside the operation theatre.

"This is all under the government's control," said Riwazzo stubbornly.

"Exactly! This invariably means that all the resources are already in place. All I have to do is press a button," replied Burburry, pushing his hands again into his pockets, as if he could surpass their original depth and dig further inside. Burburry blushed at the brilliance of his own thought without hesitation or shame.

"And you want me to make more of the 'evolution virus'?" asked Riwazzo.

"Tons of it," said Burburry jovially. "As much as you can."

"How do you seek to sell it to the common public? This stuff needs to be tested. As of now, we don't know what else it can cause or do," said Riwazzo. His tone was heavy with perplexity.

"Yes. Think of the unlimited potential and opportunity. And what will be a better way to test it, than by testing it on public, which is both common and aplenty."

Riwazzo paused for a moment. He bit his lower lip while assessing Burburry's offer in his mind.

"We'll need more zombies," he finally said.

"We'll create them, my boy," replied Burburry. "We'll create as many you want."

Sebastian had now spent more than a month at the Stillwater Counselling Centre.

It was time to go home, they told him.

'Which home are they talking about?' he asked himself.

The government had seized what was left of his. Now they wanted to ship him off to some uncultured part of the country, whatever they could get for a low price.

And then what?

For the foreseeable future, he would be stuck in America, holding himself up to the expectations of the outside world. Who would listen or pay attention to people trapped in a prison? What kind of government would they have?

Would Peru remain Peru or a new South America would emerge? Would a new, united continent take shape?

No, Sebastian thought sadly, this couldn't be called home now.

He was feeling disheartened when Dr. Grace Arborea told him he had a visitor.

The doctor, who looked rather smitten at the moment, was usually very professional in her dealings. She was thirty-six, with pale blonde hair and a soft demeanour, and was far too intelligent to look like a breathless school girl of twelve, Sebastian thought.

The visitor turned out to be a member of The Security Detail, the brave group of volunteers who were there to save America.

Sebastian was sitting in the cafeteria and the doctor offered to escort the soldier there. Sebastian felt a pang of jealousy, which the good doctor would report as a very good sign.

He waited while Dr. Grace scuttled out of the cafeteria to fetch the probably too-handsome-for-his-own-good military man.

A few minutes later, a young man in a khaki uniform with plenty of pockets, wearing regulation army boots strode into the cafeteria. He was followed by Dr. Grace, who as Sebastian could see, was trying her best to maintain her composure.

Sebastian could see her blush and her skin looked lovelier than usual in its dewy pink hue.

"Ah, here he is, the famous recluse," she said as she pointed at the only person seated in the cafeteria at the time.

The army man stopped midway and waited politely for Dr. Grace to leave them two alone, which, to Sebastian's ill-concealed astonishment, she did.

Dr. Grace walked out of the cafeteria, taking extra-large steps. She was nodding professionally at no one in particular, probably to herself.

Rocky turned around and walked briskly towards Sebastian's table.

"Sergeant Sidharth Singhania," he introduced himself with an easy smile as he shook Sebastian's hand.

Sebastian got up from the table and returned the gesture, a bit hesitantly.

"Nice to meet you, Sergeant. What can I do for you?" he asked while he was still standing.

Rocky requested Sebastian to take his seat. He sat across the table in a professional but relaxed manner.

"This is about a small matter regarding which the military would like you to help," he said.

"Sure Sergeant, what is it?"

"Well, we are rounding up locals like yourself... by which I mean people who lived through the worse phase of the apocalypse, people who are still recovering from it."

"What do you want us to do?" Sebastian enquired politely.

"Nothing at all," replied Rocky stroking his hair, a habit he thought he had conquered long back, which had now resurfaced. He tried his best to look concerned as he mustered on.

"We need your help to fill-in a few blank spots in our narrative, help us understand what really happened," he finished apologetically.

Sebastian, who had thought that the government had come to ask him to leave, felt relieved to the core. He took a deep breath as he shrugged the anxiety off his mind.

"Sure," he replied brightly, feeling obliged towards the military man.

"It's settled then," said Rocky, getting up from his seat with a wide smile on his face. "We'll see you at 6:00 a.m. tomorrow."

He shook hands with Sebastian and said goodbye.

Matt landed at Stillwater Airport where a Humvee was ready to ferry him to Stillwater University.

Bart Romney, the famed microbiologist at New York University was there to greet him at the university campus.

"We've taken over the university labs," he said as he walked Matt inside the university doors.

And that was when Matt ran into Sebastian.

Sebastian walked past him without noticing who it was. He was accompanied by a handsome young fellow in a military green uniform.

"Sebastian," Matt shouted in delight. He couldn't believe his eyes.

Sebastian turned.

Sebastian had been one of a handful of survivors. At least from amongst those who had stayed behind. He had refused to contact anyone he knew from Stillwater, who might still be alive.

Matt had presumed he was dead.

Sebastian extended his arm to shake hands with Matt, but Matt just came forward and hugged him tight. Real tight. They were meeting after months. It certainly seemed like it had been a really long time since America had been quarantined. Matt's hug was soothing to Sebastian after his unending suffering ever since the zombie outbreak had begun and he had lost his family. He remembered shooting his own sister with a shotgun. A warm embrace from a friend had brought back his memory in sporadic but vivid flashes.

When they both released each other, both of them had tears brimming in their eyes. They were overwhelmed to find someone from the family after everything had seemed so long-lost and forlorn. The unexpected meeting filled their hearts with contentment, after a long time.

"Everything okay?" asked Sebastian.

"Everyone's safe," Matt replied. "And you?" he asked instinctively.

Sebastian hung his head low, morose.

Matt wanted to hug him again.

Rocky gave Sebastian a pat on the shoulder with a smile. "He's a survivor, our boy," said Rocky.

"What are you doing here?" Sebastian asked suddenly.

Bart clucked his tongue. "This really is top secret," he interjected.

"I'll handle this," said Rocky turning towards Sebastian.

"This man," said Rocky, gesturing towards Matt with a wave of his arm, "has been brought for tests. We are developing a cure for the zombie virus. We are very close to inventing one, actually."

Bart looked unhappy.

"Yes," said Matt. "In fact, I'm immune to the virus now. Isn't that right, Professor?"

"Yes," Bart was forced to reply. "But we still need you for further tests."

"Awww professor," said Rocky. "Can't he get the day off? Considering these two have just met."

Rocky looked at both of them with fatherly affection.

"I'll give them a proper tour of the facility."

Bart gave Rocky a look which said, 'I hope you know what you are doing.'

"The military knows best," Bart said aloud. "I'll see you

tomorrow morning then," he said to Matt. "Sergeant Sidharth here will show you to the quarters we have prepared for your stay."

"Sure professor," said Rocky cheerfully, with a mock salute.

"It would be good to catch up," said Matt.

Bart walked away making a disgusted sound.

"Would you like to see how close we've come to a cure?" Rocky announced casually, like a magician conjures a rabbit out of his hat.

Research on the cure, Rocky told them, was taking place in an underground facility for certain reasons. But he didn't elaborate and led them out of the university doors instead.

The campus which used to be full of students, was now occupied by military personnel. The bags and hearty laughter of students was replaced with check-posts and barricades, barbed wires and guns.

Rocky weaved through them expertly, keeping up a constant banter about the cure.

"It's more than a cure," he boasted. "It allows one to evolve and think above the ordinary and mundane. It makes us more adaptive to the external environment we thrive in. The cure or Locker as it is famously called, is soothing to our souls. Like a tranquiliser which makes us adjust better to our surroundings"

He looked jealously at Matt.

"You mean you haven't been given the cure?" asked Sebastian surprised. He figured the military would be the first ones to receive the cure. Guess he might have been wrong.

"It's still in its beta stage," said Rocky glibly. "Meant only for high ranking officers and what not," he said and winked. "Still, I've heard it's a wonderful thing," he continued after a pause, "to be at peace."

"Have you ever suffered from depression?" he asked Matt and Sebastian.

"No," lied Sebastian, wondering when would he get to spend time and catch up with Matt. Rocky wouldn't let either of them get a word in edgeways.

"Hahahaha," laughed Rocky. "Still the cure is a wonderful thing, I hear," he added in a conspiratorial whisper.

"Anyway, here we are," he said as they reached the entrance to the subway.

"Here?" asked Sebastian in bewilderment. "Inside the subway station?"

"Yup," answered Rocky with a mock bow.

"Why all the security?" asked Matt.

The entrance to the subway was heavily guarded. They even had military personnel wearing flamethrower suits while others were carrying anti-tank weapons.

"Secrets," replied Rocky mysteriously.

He set out towards the subway entrance. Sebastian and Matt had no choice but to follow him.

Everything inside the metro station seemed intact.

They crossed the ticket counters.

Rocky jumped over the turnstiles like a trained acrobat and gestured Matt and Sebastian to follow.

The escalators were still working. They rode them down in silence.

"Et voila," exclaimed Rocky, as the underground platforms came into view.

Sebastian widened his eyes in disbelief and realised what unlimited resources meant when he saw what the government had done inside the station.

The underground stations were these huge cavernous spaces. This one, once occupied by two tracks on either side of a very broad platform, had been replaced by a large thick structure made of highly reinforced steel, which sat in the middle of the underground space. The structure was circular at the bottom with a large door at its centre. The dome on top resembled a beehive with windows at regular intervals. It was made of glass which was thicker and stronger than steel.

The whole thing seemed impenetrable. Like it had been designed to keep something out. Or protect something inside. Nothing would breach those strong walls. Nothing.

The doors at the base of the structure were approximately two feet thick. They were open and unguarded.

The cool blast of the air conditioner made Sebastian realise he was sweating.

Rocky motioned for them to follow him as he walked through the massive doors. As Sebastian entered inside the doors and into the belly of the structure, he felt afraid. Not of anything real. But the fear bit him and turned his mouth to salt.

After making their way through the doors, they entered a spacious waiting area with sliding glass doors at the far end. One hemispherical igloo-like structure stood at the centre of the room. A few seats lined either side of the walls.

The igloo in the centre looked more like an ice cream station, thought Sebastian, and was manned by two people. One was a red-haired woman in her forties and another was a young man in his early twenties. Both of them wore lab coats and looked overworked. Relentless hours of work in the laboratory had made hollow dents under her eyes. What was the military doing, buried deep inside the ground? It made Sebastian very curious.

Rocky waved at the redhead enthusiastically.

She nodded in return, curtly.

Sebastian couldn't help smiling.

The redhead pressed a button and the glass doors behind her slid open.

Rocky gestured at Sebastian and Matt, asking them to move towards the room.

Matt had not said anything all this while. This surprised Sebastian. Matt was mostly insecure about a lot of things and often made conversation to hide it. Under the present circumstances, he should have been chirping like a grasshopper.

But today, there was a focus to him, a determination, a presence which was hard to shake off.

Sebastian felt that he could trust him. He felt safe around him.

They stepped through the glass doors which closed behind them.

They were inside a rectangular room which was roughly half the size of shipping container. There were frosted glass doors a few feet in front of them, which were closed.

Sebastian heard the sound of suppressed air hissing into the room along with the smell of disinfectant.

A few seconds later, the doors in front of them opened.

"A superficial precaution," said Rocky as he led the way forward.

They entered a large room, the size of a football field.

It was packed with multiple cubicles. And each cubicle was manned by a person in a lab coat.

"The heart of the operation?" asked Sebastian a little rudely. He was getting tired of all this magician business. Enough was enough. He didn't want to be shown things. He was too tired for that.

Rocky who had begun making his way through the aisles between the cubicles, turned around and laughed. "Not really. You haven't seen anything yet."

Matt said nothing but he looked troubled. Sebastian wanted him to speak. He wanted to know if Matt was as curious, rather suspicious of this secret, underground mission of the government as Sebastian was.

They walked along the east wall of the room, passing several doors on their way. Most doors had a plaque with a person's name on it. There was a conference room, a pantry and at the far end, Sebastian could see signs for the toilets.

Halfway down the hall they came in front of a pair of wide steel doors. Rocky pulled out a card and waved it at the sensor fitted in the wall next to the doors. The sensor was fitted with a bright green LED which blazed and confirmed Rocky's ID. Sebastian was wondering about the number of doors which they were yet to get through. What was it that awaited them in the end?

The doors slid open, slick and well-oiled.

"In here," said Rocky as he ducked through the doorway.

Sebastian hesitated. Then he glanced around at all the people working around him and told himself he was being silly. It was safe in here. Even more than when he was outside.

He followed Rocky, and Matt followed him.

They entered a large corridor. This is where the tracks must have been once, Sebastian thought to himself.

One side of the corridor was made of glass. The same thick glass Sebastian had noticed on the windows. The other side was steel behind which the cubicle workers sat.

They turned right and walked further down through the corridor.

"This is one of the metro tunnels," said Rocky. He smiled widely as he urged Sebastian and Matt to take the lead.

Sebastian walked in front, then Rocky. Matt followed silently, as if he was being forced into a chamber of secrets he just didn't want to unearth.

The corridor looked like an underwater aquarium, sans all the fish of course.

They were now walking down the metro tunnel surrounded by glass on both sides. The only steel that remained was underfoot.

Even the ceiling was made of glass.

It was then that Sebastian realised what the government had done. His realisation terrified him.

He looked outside the glass and though he had expected it, he still couldn't believe his eyes. All he could see were zombies. In hordes, running along the glass corridor, throwing themselves at it the moment they laid eyes on the humans inside. Sebastian was petrified. Despite of being safe behind the thick glass walls, the blood inside his legs curdled with fear. He could recall the bloodied encounter which had left his entire family dead, and him, devastated.

The tunnel was full of them. They swarmed like bees in a hive. Like a catastrophe, fighting each other, desperate to attack the humans.

"This corridor is continuous and runs through all the underground tracks of Stillwater," Rocky paused and announced. "Soon we'll be coming up to the next station."

Sebastian watched in revulsion as the creatures continued to attack the glass, trying to bite it, trying to bite the humans behind it.

He turned around. Rocky had drawn a gun.

"You see, like always, it starts with money." He stepped back and gestured for Matt to stand next to Sebastian.

"All this was built for one reason and one reason alone," he continued waving his free hand around the corridor, "to harness what is being referred by scientists as the 'de-evolution' virus."

Rocky laughed again. The same old laughter, the same lovely eyes, but with a hint of sarcasm in them. He knew something they didn't. Rocky had always known something other people didn't. It had made him the way he was now.

"The virus can be extracted only from the zombies and so we had to keep them... Aren't they beautiful?"

He paused.

"You might be curious about what will happen next," he continued. "Well, gentlemen," he said pointing at the large steel doors set in the glass wall, "this is your stop."

Next to the heavy doors was a complicated looking mechanism on the wall to its right.

"It is like the doors in a space shuttle," said Rocky after a moment or two. "On the other side of these doors is a small chamber followed by another set of doors. Both set of doors are never opened together, for obvious reasons."

"The objective of the chamber is to trap a zombie. For that I need only open the second set of doors, wait for the zombie to step inside the room and then close the doors behind it. Then we can draw whatever we need from it. After knocking it unconscious, of course." Sebastian stared at him in horror now.

"Call it an 'in tray'." Rocky's smile had turned hard now. Like the one on a butcher's face before the slaughter.

"But," and here Rocky paused heavily for effect, "the process also works in reverse."

He ordered Matt and Sebastian to stand aside and flashed a card at the door. He operated a lever, pressed a button and the door opened.

"Gentlemen," he said. Sebastian and Matt walked through.

"Good luck," he said. And then the doors closed.

The chamber was the size of an elevator. A few seconds later, the doors in front of Matt and Sebastian began to open.

The first thing that came through the opened doors was the stench. The familiar smell of blood, shit and decaying skin made Sebastian gag in fear.

And the noise. He had not forgotten it. He never would. But he had also never imagined he would hear it again.

The screeching, the howling. The thumping. The madness.

Sebastian was back in his apartment once more. Trembling and waiting for the inevitable. So death had caught up with him after all.

The first zombie dashed headlong towards Sebastian. A young, sturdy man, almost naked, matted all over with filth. It jumped as it reached its hands towards Sebastian's neck.

Sebastian tried to grab its face as it sprang at him, but his hands missed. He groped the zombie's chest ineffectively while the zombie caught hold of him around the waist and bit him on the shoulder as they both fell over.

Matt stood back in a corner of the elevator. The zombie that had rushed towards Sebastian was one of three. Two others were also screeching and running towards the open door of the chamber.

Matt peed inside his pants. Just as the warmth of fresh piss hit his body, the two zombies charged into the elevator.

A twenty something woman in a tattered black skirt, naked on top, slammed into him.

The breath knocked out of him, crushed between the woman and the shut door behind him, Matt waited for the inevitable bite.

But it never came.

The woman took a step backward, uncertainly. Matt looked her in the eyes and saw no signs of humanity. She was indifferent, oblivious. The one goal she knew was to infect and kill.

The woman then looked down at Sebastian's prone form, which the young sturdy zombie had left behind.

Then she turned around and went out back the way she had come from. The other zombie, which had stopped short as soon as it had entered the chamber, stayed for a few moments and then it too left.

Before Matt's mind could process what had just happened, Sebastian's eyes opened. Only they weren't Sebastian's eyes anymore. He was not himself anymore. He had turned into a zombie.

The zombie slowly got up, staring at Matt. Then it turned suddenly to face the door. With bird-like movements, it began to walk towards the exit.

It was through the door when Matt shouted in desperation, "Sebastian!"

The zombie paused for a second. Then it began walking again.

"What the hell," said Matt and followed it.

"What do you mean you released him?" asked Romney, a furious shade of purple.

"There wasn't any time to tag them," replied Rocky.

"Tag them? You idiot! One of them was injected with the evolution virus."

"Yeah, I know. So?" asked Rocky with a savage look on his face.

"The zombie bug won't affect him. They won't bite him." Romney was livid, spluttering and shouting.

"He was compromised the minute he met Sebastian. Do you know Sebastian saw us loading zombies into the chopper before De Gaulle's virus was released? He had started telling people about it." Rocky smiled.

"You've infected the entire population, every study," said Bart, full of rage.

"Will he survive?" asked Rocky dispassionately, with idle curiosity.

"Who knows? This has never been done before. Obviously," added Bart dryly.

"Will he eat what we give them to eat?" asked Rocky.

"He'll have to. Now what do I tell my superiors?"

"Do you have to say anything at all?" asked Rocky, innocently. Romney looked at Rocky for a minute. "No, I guess it will not be necessary," he said finally.

Two years later...

The voice rang loud and clear. "Radha," the voice said, "you are doing it again."

Radha broke free from her moment and frowned.

"I told you not to do that," repeated her mom.

"But mom," Radha felt like saying. Instead she let out an audible sigh.

Her mom was explaining her recipe for pan seared tuna to her sister on the phone.

Radha got up and left the kitchen. Her mom and sister would go on for hours on the phone, preparing dinner for their respective families.

"How can she ask me not to lock when I have to hear her go on like that?"

The drug wasn't illegal. In fact, the great Bart Romney, the rebel chief, advocated its use.

Anybody in America who even remotely claimed to be pro-evacuation couldn't deny that Bart himself used the drug. The Locker was the chief produce of 'New America' as the continent was now being called.

"And if I have children, I'll let them lock as well," said Radha to herself as she crossed the street and went out into the park to be by herself.

She sat down on a swing and took out a vial from her pocket; one of only three, she noted dispassionately.

She broke open the vial and inhaled it deeply.

Then she pushed the ground with her feet and waited for her mind to latch on to a particular thought as she swung to and fro. Her mind, with all its ferocious intensity, held on. For a few hours, she stayed in a state of single-minded bliss. Then she widened her thoughts again. The process of narrowing and widening, which would normally have taken a few seconds, minutes at best, had been extended to a few hours. Radha felt happy, much better now.

She sighed and got up.

Her Dad must be home by now. Her step-dad. Radha had started walking back towards her apartment.

"You of all people shouldn't take the Locker, Radha" her stepfather reprimanded her.

They were all sitting at the dining table of their New York apartment. It was tiny but cosy, thought James.

"No Dad, I do not want to hear about another conspiracy theory," said Radha and made a face. She loved the Locker, this new tranquilising drug which was harmless, but pacified her for hours at a stretch.

Hillary was about to say something, but James stopped her. He was not finished talking yet.

James was a university professor and taught philosophy at New York University. He was short, stout and wore large, black-rimmed spectacles, which kept slipping off his nose. The only thing he took pride in as far as his appearance was concerned was, his thick, lustrous hair which fell down his sides.

"It's not a conspiracy theory, Radha," said James. "People have been disappearing. It's got something to do with this drug. Sure it widens the mind. But what good is it?"

"So you think I'll widen my mind so much that I disappear too?" asked Radha. She almost laughed, but didn't want an outburst from her mom. If James, or Jimmy as her mother referred to him, wanted to preach, let him.

"Do you know New America's chief export? No? It's the Locker. This drug is the reason the world continues to keep us under quarantine. Why do you think a quarantine is still necessary? Do you really think Bart is on our side? No, the drug can only be produced under conditions of quarantine. Don't you wonder why?" James thought he had gone too far this time. Radha wasn't a child. An eight-year-old wasn't a child in the world they lived in. Humanity had evolved too quickly for its own good.

"They'll still get it once we're free." Radha chuckled, now enjoying the conversation.

"No, they won't. You mark my words. It's made from the zombie bug!" Now James was shouting.

"They say it resembles the zombie bug in many ways. But you don't have to worry. I've never felt as evolved as when I take the Locker."

"Honey, it's not that," said Hillary. "We know the drug is perfectly safe." She gave James a warning glance.

The drug in question was known on the streets as 'the Locker'. It had surfaced in America a few months after the zombie outbreak which was the source of its inspiration, as claimed by its patent holder, Dr. Riwazzo.

It had become popular in the New America, and had spread outwards into the world, although its use outside of New America was illegal.

New America was governed by an elected body, but in reality, took orders from Hung Ti, Japan's erstwhile Premier and now businessman along with Ray Burburry. Together they were the single largest holder of property in America.

James and a select group of people had made it their job to prove this. Their theory was that New America was being exploited by the rich and powerful. But the world just didn't care, they had realised.

New America was not the same as the erstwhile Unites States of America. It didn't have oil reserves at its disposal, it didn't have much of an army left, nor an air force. Its once flourishing economy was now fractured and worked on the system of rationing.

No, the great leaders of the world were not concerned about America's plight. America did not lead the world anymore.

Matt opened his eyes. It was morning, and he knew this because of the feeding cycle followed by the laboratory staff which was Matt's only indication of time.

He was thirty-seven, but his body looked grey and wasted.

He jogged for thirty minutes, twice a day. He would choose two stations at random and jog between them, once in the morning when he awoke and once in the evening, before feeding time.

As he would reach the doors of each station, he would imagine he was with his daughter and he would shout loudly, "Whisletown St., honey."

But instead of his daughter's excited squeal, he would hear the screeching of zombies, a jarring sound which stayed on the nerves long after.

It wasn't as if they were trying to communicate. It was more like they were venting.

He would tie Sebastian to the tracks while he exercised. As time had moved on, Matt had come to realise that Sebastian was something less than human. A creature that had no wants of its own but followed solely the dictates of the virus.

Matt, who had been a jock in college, had taken to his fitness regime with ease. It gave him something to do. Something to look forward to.

But the lack of daylight had taken its toll. His skin was cracking and peeling in places. It was hard to distinguish him from a zombie, except that they died faster.

The zombie cycle of death in the underground metro network

was well known to Matt. It consisted of not getting enough to eat, getting thin, not being able to fight to survive and eventually getting eaten by other stronger zombies.

Matt had promised himself he would not suffer the same fate. Nor let Sebastian. He made sure that Sebastian was well fed, but Sebastian had not shown any qualities of being a pet. His eyes were still yellow, still watchful. He treated Matt with complete indifference and unconcern, even while eating the food provided by Matt.

He would have attacked and eaten Matt had Matt not been stronger. But then, Matt had always been stronger.

Where food was concerned, the zombies never knew what they would get to eat.

Some days it was just food which consisted of raw meat or fish. But on special occasions, they would get a human to bite and infect.

Matt had yet not got used to the frenzy and the noises they would make on such an occasion.

More zombies were being added on a regular basis as the old ones died or were eaten. The total number of zombies was always at a healthy maximum.

Matt had waited for company. But they had never sent one like him over here, inside the facility. Those tests were conducted inside the laboratories, beyond steel doors.

The same steel doors that Matt lounged about every day. Different stations, different laboratories, but the huge steel doors remained constant, omnipresent.

Matt had never had the courage to walk through them. To be the zombie they took back for tests. Because, he reasoned, once they gassed him with chloroform in the chamber, he might never wake up again.

But the time was coming when he thought he would be

desperate enough to try it. When death would become an acceptable cost for his escape.

The only reason Matt kept Sebastian around him was to remind himself of the person he'd once been. 'A sorry reminder,' thought Matt as he watched Sebastian screech at a little girl who screeched back in alarm.

Matt tugged at the cord around his foot. The cord was made of cloth, a white shirt now brown with use. The other end was tied to the leg of the zombie that had once been Sebastian.

Matt had tied the cloth to Sebastian two years ago. Now Sebastian followed Matt out of habit. But at night, Matt still tied the cloth. Losing Sebastian would mean losing his only connection, his only reminder of the world outside. He'd become as much animal as the ones he lived with. Matt's agony seemed never-ending. The government had tricked them both into the experiment. Matt and Sebastian were nothing but guinea pigs. There was no escape from this situation, no matter how hard they tried.

But as far as animals go, zombies were a disappointment. They developed no habits, no cooperation, no means of communication. They were neither animal, nor man; they were completely ruined creatures, oblivious to sanity or emotion.

Once you took procreation out of the equation, a species just grew old and died. They were more like single-celled organisms, like bacteria or a virus.

Matt had figured out the lie. He had understood, even as he saw more zombies being added and some being subtracted, that the zombies were being harnessed for something. A weapon?

It kept him awake at night, knowing that someone was making more zombies and still not being able to do a thing about it.

Perhaps it was the only reason he was still sane. The wretched helplessness of it all would come to his aid just as he was sure he would go mad.

And no matter how much he clawed his head in the dark solitary night, the helplessness would give his mind something to do.

Maybe someday, someone, somewhere would discover this ugly secret. And then Matt could walk out a free man.

But till that happened, the only way out stared him in the face, like a game of Russian roulette.

Bart Romney had captured the hearts and imagination of almost everybody in the world. He was working tirelessly for the cause of those who had been quarantined.

Once a champion for the government, he had now only the best interest of the people at the very core of his heart.

"The way out," he would say on TV, brandishing the Locker virus in one hand, "was hope."

Which, Hung Ti, the erstwhile Japanese Premier, said was a pack of lies.

He claimed that businesses in America were corrupt and had established a monopoly over the artificial economy. He neglected to mention he was one of them.

He further iterated that the process of aid-giving and rehabilitation, which had been placed in the hands of the military, was being in fact funded by some very powerful people.

Several Japanese teams had already made incursions into the United States, incursions that meant a permanent stay of residence in order to prove these accusations.

Nothing had changed except that there were now more military personnel in America.

"Without depression, there is no barrier to your ability to react." James was standing at the podium of the large amphitheatre. It was his favourite time of the day. Teaching contemporary philosophy.

"You can evolve supremely. Depression, you see, is simply the inability to react. The inability to understand. Take in information. Now a drug that allows you to interact limitlessly with the world around you is excellent. Only that it causes depression in turn." His voice was booming in the pin-drop silence.

"I mean, you can only interact with the world a certain degree and not be depressed. After a point, it is the very interaction with the world that causes depression. No drug could sustain an increase in the rate of evolution. And isn't it convenient? Answer me this. You all know evolution is necessary. So why speed it up?"

Nobody said a word, so he continued, "No, the Locker is bound to fail. It will remain just as useless and just as cheap as any other drug in the market."

James cleared his throat, hoping he had made his point clear and succinct.

Zombies or no zombies, the drug was bound to fail.

He took one last glance at his class of young bright minds, forced to live under quarantine in a nation devoid of scruples, and decided that he would do something about it.

He was on his way home from the NYU. For better or worse, Hillary had made her temporary residence in New York her permanent address. It was then when he thought of something. What if he visited Stillwater? That would be doing something. Surely. He could see where the epidemic had started. He could visit the Grand Library.

Stillwater University was now under military occupation; it had been for some time now.

And the government had the best resources. The library was no exception. There were all kinds of records of the apocalypse which were not available throughout the country, nay the world.

James was twenty-seven, highly successful in his field, and extremely ambitious. But he wasn't particularly good looking with a squat face and a flat nose. The fact that he was short, 5'7" or thereabouts, didn't help matters much either.

Which was why he was surprised when a beauty like Hillary fell into his lap.

They met at a protest arranged by Bart Romney. Bart had set Hillary up with a nice compensation for the loss of her husband, and Hillary, in exchange, had begun working for him. Mostly because she had nothing else to do.

Bridget had been in charge of educating Radha.

But after Hillary and James had moved in together, Hillary had asked her in-laws to move out and find an apartment of their own.

James had been living in her apartment for a year now.

He asked Hillary for her opinion over dinner.

Hillary watched Radha fondly as Radha forked a potato.

"Well, if you think you should... I can't say no. I don't want to say yes, but I can't say no either."

James was surprised when support came from an unexpected ally. "I'll go with you," said Radha, of all people.

"And who invited you?" asked Hillary.

Then she caught James' glance.

'It would be a good way for us to bond,' his eyes said.

"Why do you even want to come?" he asked Radha.

Radha smiled knowing she had won. "I just want to see my home one more time."

There was no arguing with such a sincere emotional response.

"When do you leave?" she asked.

"The day after tomorrow. The flight leaves in the afternoon. We should get there by early evening. We'll stay there over the weekend and catch the flight back to New York on Sunday evening, in time for you to go to school."

"I'm on my summer vacation," Radha protested.

James laughed.

Hillary had a bad feeling about his plan.

A few months ago, Radha had established contact with Bart.

It had been over the internet where she had been following him for a while. To tell the truth, she had developed a crush on him when Hillary had been working for him.

But it was only after she had mentioned the name Ray Burburry, that Bart had started taking an interest in her. A name James had mentioned a couple of times at the dinner table.

'It pays to listen,' Radha had proudly texted Bart after their first little exchange.

Bart has responded with a smiley faced emoticon.

Since then, they had become close friends. Bart would listen patiently to all of Radha's problems while asking her random questions about what James talked about on the dinner table.

Once, Bart had become so excited he had called her an ingenious little idiot for which he had later profusely apologized.

She had been telling Bart that she had overheard James talking to somebody on the phone in Japanese. She was sure because of the Japanese greeting, 'Koh-ni-chua.'

James was nervous about the whole thing. What was he going to find there? Was it merely a hobby? Was he indulging himself in a pre-mid-life crisis?

He had known it to happen to many people of his age. The stress of over-achievement, a sort of emptiness and disappointment with the world around.

Radha hugged herself and reread her conversations with Bart. She didn't have any Locker with her because of airport security.

Hopefully she'd find some in Stillwater.

She had told her parents that she had wanted to visit her old house. It had been an excuse she had made up at the spur of the moment and one she was proud of. But now that she was actually going back to Stillwater, she was more than a little curious about how her old home looked. After the zombies had been through it.

They landed at Stillwater Airport at 7:00 p.m. James went up and started chatting with the woman at the Starbucks counter, while they were waiting for their bags to show up on the conveyor.

At first Radha thought he was flirting with her. But upon closer inspection she observed that they were talking like old friends, or at least old acquaintances. Maybe the woman at the Starbucks counter was one of *them*.

Bart had told her to keep an eye out for anybody James talked to who was not from the university. Especially if they were Japanese.

In Radha's mind, a huge tale had already taken shape.

About Bart, who was good and heroic, against whom James and his secret group of co-conspirators were plotting.

They needed to be taught a lesson and they would be, he had promised her.

Radha's suspicions were confirmed when James returned without a coffee.

She decided not to bring up that matter lest she alert him to her mission.

She would be a good spy and text Bart about the woman once they were back in New York. Meanwhile, she would keep her eyes and ears open.

James guided her towards the exit and flagged a cab.

He booked two small rooms at an average hotel; the most he could afford when he went gallivanting after a whim, he told himself.

They had dinner in their respective rooms. The rooms were small and clean, but room service was slow. Radha almost shouted at the gentleman from house keeping when he failed to turn on the hot water in the bathroom. She was tired and wanted to take a bath after a long day.

How quickly the facade of family falls apart, James thought bitterly as he dug into his pasta carbonara. He would visit the library early in the morning tomorrow. The Grand Library opened at 6:00 a.m., in accordance with military regulation.

If Radha wanted to come with him, she could wander around inside the university campus. Otherwise, she could visit her old home. Since Stillwater was a military zone, crime rate was zero. It was quite safe. Still, thought James, he could wrangle out a favour from an old contact in the military and get Radha an escort, to ensure that she would be absolutely safe.

He fell asleep thinking about the next day.

In the other room, Radha made her plans. She would finally get a chance to meet the great Bart Romney. She had so much to ask him about. So much to tell him about her life.

It was going to be wonderful.

Early in the morning, they set off for Stillwater University together in a cab.

Sarah, the woman behind the coffee counter, had told James that he would require special permission to get inside the university. The military guarded it earnestly, along with some private security personnel. There were guard dogs and barbed wires spread across every inch of the campus.

Fortunately, a high-rank person from the bureaucracy, sympathetic to their cause, had done the paperwork for James.

The cab stopped at the first checkpoint and James got off with Radha.

The card worked like magic, thought James as they crossed their third and final checkpoint without a single question asked.

Radha was impressed, in spite of her air of indifference for James which she had carefully cultivated during the last one year.

The university was a lot like Capitol Hill in Washington. The same wide, white-marbled steps; the same kind of doors, large and imposing.

James waked through the university doors, with Radha in tow.

He entered the high-ceilinged lobby and went towards the woman sitting behind a large and deep desk.

"The Grand Library," he asked with a smile he couldn't help.

The woman at the reception gave him half a glance and pointed to her left and went back to the paperback she was reading.

James took Radha's hand in his and started in the direction the receptionist had indicated.

Straight down the corridor, at the very end was the entrance to the Grand Library. The entrance, thought James, left a lot to be desired and imagined.

The gigantic doors of the library were larger than any other door in the university, but they were also covered with thick flecks of dirt and grime. It seemed that years of neglect had already played their hand. Though this was still one of the biggest libraries which James had seen, he wondered what Radha would make of the disuse and dust.

James was even less impressed when he went inside and saw the library. It was the size of half a football pitch from inside. Tiny considering how famed it was. But, he reminded himself, the real resource of the Grand Library, or any library for that matter, is information. And the digital archives of the Grand Library were beyond comparison.

Radha stopped at the doors. She didn't want to go inside that dull, boring place.

James turned around to talk to Radha. "Honey, if you want to explore the university, go ahead. Just don't leave the main doors. And answer your phone if I call you," he told her.

Radha nodded. She could not believe her luck.

James turned around, glad to be alone.

He went up to the nearest computer and sat down. If he had to search the archives for information on the apocalypse, where should he start from, he wondered.

He began typing.

Epicentre, zombie bug, apocalypse, he typed. The computer threw up a wealth of information for his perusal. He was a happy man now.

James got busy reading.

☣

Radha had tried finding Bart's office. But the university was just too big, and every time she started, she would get lost amid the yards and yards of corridors with doors everywhere she looked.

Finally, she decided to ask the receptionist. The receptionist smiled at her politely.

"What do you want with Professor Romney, you silly girl?" the receptionist rebuked her gently.

The receptionist was in her late twenties and could spot a schoolgirl's crush when she saw one.

Radha was not pleased with the answer. She blew a bubble with her gum and turned around.

Now what, she thought.

She would text Bart. Yes, that's what she would do. She should have thought of it earlier.

'I'm at Stillwater University,' Radha texted.

Instantly there was a reply. 'Have you reached already? Sorry I couldn't meet you. I'm out of town on some research work.'

'Ok,' replied Radha. Followed by a sad faced emoticon.

Then she brightened up.

She would tell Bart about the spy woman at Starbucks.

It was James' third consecutive day at the library.

He was now an apocalypse expert, if only by his reckoning.

He had read about all the theories that had floated regarding the origin of the drug and how all speculation had abruptly ended.

Nobody was wondering if it could strike again.

Ray had done a good job, thought James. A native of New York, James had survived the apocalypse as so many had, without meeting a single zombie.

But he had some inkling on how the country was being run. Things were too haphazard for a democracy.

Very little information came into the country and James was sure, very little was leaving. In fact, nobody in the rest of the world hardly had anything to say about the United States of America. It was an unwelcome addition to the family. The black sheep. The elephant in the room.

Yet it was the largest manufacturer of the Locker.

And it was then, on the third day, that James had an idea.

What if he could prove that New America was indeed the only manufacturer of the locker?

He knew this even without proving it.

Because he knew that the locker was made from zombies and none of the other countries shown in the company's prospectus could sustain or harbour zombies. It had to be so.

Finally, thought James. A way to prove that zombies were being used to make the locker.

He carefully went through the prospectus and made a note of the countries where the drug was allegedly made.

India. Slovakia. Thailand. United States of America.

This was going to be easy, he thought to himself.

He sent the information to Joe, his contact with the Japanese.

Next he decided that he would visit the street where it had all started. He would take Radha along. She was strong enough to handle it, he thought. After all, she hadn't been there when it had happened. She might even want to see her old house as she had claimed back at home, while planning the trip.

He wondered what she was up to. The university must be boring for a kid like her. All she did was sit at the reception blowing bubbles and texting someone on her phone.

A change would surely be good for both of them.

He went out of the Grand Library for a quick bathroom break.

As he passed the reception, he saw Radha talking to a stranger. A handsome man in military fatigues.

"It's not true, Sergeant Singhania," Radha said. She was squealing with delight.

James wondered for the umpteenth time how easy it was to win Radha's heart and how he had never been able to do it. He walked up to them.

"Officer," James said as Rocky looked up and stared at him cheerfully.

"Hi," said Rocky. "Does this little girl belong to you?" he asked.

"Yes. I'm in charge of her. Temporarily," James responded.

Radha made a face.

"Anyway," said Rocky getting up. "Glad to have met you both."

He walked down the corridor towards the Grand Library, turned a corner and was gone.

Hillary considered taking a flight and surprising James and Radha. But the time she had gotten for herself was too precious to waste on a sentiment.

But there was a nagging feeling that persisted at the back of her mind.

That day, while returning from the spa, she bumped into a Japanese man.

"Hi," he said apologizing and helping her regain her balance.

"Joe's the name. Joe Hill."

Hillary was taken aback. He was more American than she was.

"Hi Joe," she said with a cheeky smile.

"I was wondering if we could talk where we won't be overheard," Joe said.

Hillary was caught off guard.

"About what?" she managed to ask.

"About your husband and daughter and the amount of danger they are in," Joe said, casually, as if he was buying a pound of potatoes.

Hillary was about to raise her voice when Joe interrupted her. "Listen, there's a table right here. We can sit for a few seconds and talk about it or you can shout and I can walk away. You decide."

Hillary looked around. The tables of a cafe were spread out on the pavement around her. People were sitting around and talking.

Light, long conversations. Laughing.

She relaxed a little and took a seat. "Okay, now talk," she said.

"I am a Japanese agent and it should make you feel better to know that we are on your side." Hillary listened to him and didn't bat an eyelid.

"You don't seem to care or perhaps you are not aware of what your government is doing to its people," Joe continued.

Hillary said nothing.

"We know it is hard to believe, but it's true, unfortunately. The government is turning people into zombies to harness more of the evolution virus, the Locker as you know it," said Joe.

"We are sure they are hiding them inside the subway network at Stillwater. We just needed proof, until now." Hilary stared at him, almost expressionless.

"I have seen it myself," he added kindly.

"What has this got to do anything with James and Radha?" asked Hillary. Her chest tightened and gripped her heart.

"We are monitoring the situation even as we speak," replied Joe quickly. "No harm will come to either of them. We have extraction teams standing by. I'm here to tell you that we have the proof we need. I'm here to take you to safety."

He didn't look like he was going anywhere.

"Did you know that the Locker drug is the biggest selling commodity in the world?" Joe asked at length.

He sighed.

"Imagine that kind of power in the right hands…"

"The power to sit around and not do a thing?" Hillary asked, despite her situation. "To not be interested in anything at all, day and night. I think it would be better to become a zombie."

This time, Joe heard her out, without a word. "You told me

my family was being watched. Can I contact them?"

"Absolutely not. You have nothing to worry. My men will have them out long before they are in danger."

Hillary felt like getting up and striking this large, indifferent man who sat in front of her.

Instead, she watched him silently as he ordered a cup of coffee.

Sarah was tied up and a zombie was tied next to her. It was straining to get to her, but the length of chain around its neck didn't allow that much leeway. This had kept her alive, kept her human.

But the creature would keep trying, lurching and stopping short with maniacal regularity.

"You still don't know who any of the other members are?" asked Rocky patiently.

He wasn't even watching Sarah as he interrogated her.

He was on his phone texting someone and smiling.

The zombie lunged again. Sarah screamed in fear as it spat warm saliva in her face. It was only a few inches away from her.

"Nothing?" asked Rocky, still not looking up.

"I guess I'll let our friend have some fun with you then."

"No, no," Sarah broke down.

And she told him all about her friends in the covert group who had been contacted by the Japanese. About how only recently the Japanese had confirmed their theory that New America was making zombies to manufacture the Locker.

She also told him how the Japanese had promised they would conduct an inspection of all the other facilities where the Locker was supposedly being made.

Once Rocky had let the zombie loose and watched it bite Sarah, he waited for Sarah to go stark raving mad, and then closed the door behind him with a contented sigh.

He had everything that he needed right now. There was no need to keep James and the little girl alive.

James answered the doorbell just as he was getting ready to leave for Rogers Drive with a very reluctant Radha. The trip was not at all turning out like she had planned.

She hadn't met Bart yet. Sure, they had texted each other like crazy, but it was all information. Perhaps, Bart was taking the spy game a little too seriously. He had forgotten the fun and romance amid the game of exchanging secrets. Radha was disappointed in him.

And now she would have to go to her old home. She dreaded every second of it.

"Hi," Rocky said. "I was told by the university to contact you. Can I come in?"

James was a little taken aback.

"Regarding what?" he asked Rocky.

Rocky took a step closer to James who was blocking the doorway.

"How about you let me in or I pump you both with bullets?" asked Rocky.

James looked down and saw the little black revolver held in Sergeant Singhania's hand; complete with a silver-grey silencer. He held it tightly, like a part of his hand.

Radha popped out of her room, all dressed.

"Who is it?" she asked.

"I had to reschedule our meeting," Rocky was saying, "because of our Japanese friends. They had their hearts set on rescuing you."

James' head was spinning. None of this was making sense.

Radha screamed when she saw the gun and fainted immediately.

"There is enough time for conversation in the car," said Rocky politely as he cradled Radha with one arm. With the second, he buried the revolver deep into her belly.

"One false move and she's gone," Rocky told James. "Literally. I do not lie." He smiled sheepishly as he threatened James.

"Is she unwell?" asked the old lady who was riding the elevator down with them.

"Just a touch of the sun," answered Rocky smoothly. "We're taking her to see a doctor."

"Hope he's good," said the old woman.

"Oh," replied Rocky, "he's the best in the business."

James led the way out the hotel doors and saw a black van parked right at the curb.

"Inside," announced Rocky as the back door swung open.

James stepped inside the darkness and Rocky followed, closing the door behind him.

"We always get there in the end," said Rocky personably.

Radha had regained consciousness and was sitting rigid with fear.

Her eyes had a glazed look. James was afraid to touch her.

The van passed through several checkpoints till it reached the entrance to the underground metro.

Here it stopped and the side doors opened. James blinked owlishly at the bright sunlight.

Rocky led the way, followed by James, who was holding Radha's hand. At the end of the procession came one of Rocky's men. He was a stocky, broad man wearing black.

"You know, this reminds me of something," said Rocky as he jumped over the turnstile.

They reached the escalator and started riding it down.

Soon, the ugly domed structure came in view.

They walked a few paces from the escalator and were standing outside the thick, more-solid-than-ever doors. James paused, hovering over the doorway. It was Radha who pulled him inside as Rocky watched with a smile.

Rocky took them past the reception desk, not even trying to conceal his weapon.

The two receptionists inside the little igloo stared at the little procession, but dared to say or do nothing. Rocky asked them to buzz him through and that's what they did.

Rocky followed the same path as he had, countless times before. He moved past the big hall with the cubicles, through the large metal doors.

Radha walked rigidly behind Rocky, uttering a silent prayer. James walked behind her, with his head bowed.

The henchman walked behind them; he also held a gun in his hand.

And then they saw the zombies.

Wild, screeching beings who cared for nothing, not for sunshine or the night. They were not afraid of anything.

Radha didn't even look at them. She walked rigid in fear, looking straight ahead. It would have been the only time she could have boasted of seeing a zombie.

It appeared she had reached some safe place deep inside and would stay there.

James' mind was whirring, while thinking of one hasty plan after another. But he too kept walking, not looking at the creatures which ran around them. The zombies were separated by a glass wall so thick that it could withstand the weight of several elephants easily.

After fifteen minutes or so of this madness, Rocky brought them to a halt.

He stood by a pair of metallic doors with a wolfish smile on his lips. The sadist in him rejoiced at what was going to happen.

"I think a little show and tell is in order," he said, enjoying every second.

"Now I will open the inner door," and he pressed a button on the panel next to the doors and the doors sunk into the glass panel to his right.

"Now you get in," he said, gesturing at James and Radha.

James knew, though the thought was somewhere at the back of his mind, that Radha was immune to the zombies. Never having tried the Locker himself, he knew he wasn't.

During the last three days, he had read up extensively on the zombie apocalypse. He knew what zombies did to the little ones. The weak ones.

"Now," gestured Rocky, a little impatiently.

There was already a mass of zombies swelling at the outer doors of the chamber.

Waiting. They knew what would happen next.

James pretended as if he would walk through the doors. Radha followed. But just as he passed the panel, he lunged and struck the red button, next to the one which Rocky had just pressed.

Plain dumb luck and some simple engineering skills were with him that day. Although James would not live to appreciate it.

Rocky's gun made a sound like a nail being driven into a lump of wood as he shouted, "You fool!"

James' body was pitched against the panel as the bullet smashed through his chest and came out through his back. It struck the glass panel and fell on the steel floor with a clatter. The outer doors opened slowly and the frenzied horde of zombies now charged through.

The henchman who was not immune to the zombie bug turned on his heels and ran with unsightly haste, back the way he had come.

The zombies ignored both Rocky and Radha as they charged up the tunnel, looking for untainted humans.

"Damn you, bitch!" Rocky snarled at Radha and raised his revolver. Radha closed both her eyes tight.

Nothing happened.

She opened her eyes. Rocky was lying on the floor, unconscious.

And a dirty, smelly, tattered Matt stood over him.

Matt. Her father.

Matt looked at her and smiled through cracked lips and yellow teeth.

"Hi honey," he managed to whisper.

She stood there for a whole second before she ran into his arms.

Then she noticed that he was tied to something.

"Sebastian," Matt mouthed though he realised it would be kinder to let go of the zombie who had once been Sebastian.

He'd seen it happen before. Death would come slowly and violently.

Nobody stood a chance once the zombies grouped against you; man, woman or even a giant like Rocky.

Rocky was awake now, only to find zombies clamouring over him and biting into his entire body, from top to bottom.

He sat up and tried shaking them off. He yelled in pain as one of them bit him hard on the left ear.

Rock was drenched in blood and more spurted out with each bite. He was strong, but the zombies were too many to be overpowered and too hungry and crazed to ever stop.

He died screaming in agony as they tore his stomach into pieces and bit into his soft insides while they held him down, under their combined weight.

Matt covered Radha's eyes and walked away with her.

China was angry. At least the Chinese Premier Zedong was.

"A tour of inspection is the least that we demand," he said and banged his fist on the table.

"Yes, of course. That's easy," lied the American President on the monitor, "but you know this is a delicate matter. Industry secrets.

"They don't matter anymore. We have the backing of the United Nations. Ratified. None of these facilities have the right to bar us entry."

"Are you accusing me of something?" asked Charles.

"We will soon see," replied Premier Wen.

Charles switched off the monitor. He wiped the beads of sweat from his forehead.

It had begun on the day of the outbreak. Hung Ti had called him.

"Congratulations, Charles." Hung Ti said.

Why?"

"You haven't figured it out? It's our virus, the one that was supposed to cure depression. Remember what it did, the virus? It was supposed to remove people's inability to react to external stimuli. What if it did the exact opposite?" Ti had said.

"What? That's not possible!"

"Do you know something that I don't, because this just doesn't make sense to me," replied Charles though he had begun to

148

understand only too well.

"What I'm saying is that you have to stay put. Not evacuate. And we'll both be rich men."

"You're out of your mind."

"Do you know where we tested that anti-depression virus?"

Charles realised he knew the answer.

Stillwater, Oklahoma.

Looking back, he still thought he had gotten the raw side of the deal. And now there was this inspection coming up with pressure from all sides of the world. He was being questioned. He was on their radar. The country which once ruled the roost and dominated global politics was on its knees.

The Japanese government wouldn't help. Not against the Chinese. The Chinese were quite capable of using nuclear weapons if not given their way. Stocky little bastards, murmured Charles, clenching his fist so tight that he almost cried out in pain.

The phone rang again. Just as it had, all those years ago. Charles knew who it was.

Hung Ti; the man Charles had betrayed when he'd signed up with Ray all those years ago.

"Hi Charles," said Hung Ti.

"What do we do?" asked Charles, once more the protege.

"It's simple Charles. I'm surprised the idea didn't occur to you."

"What is it?"

"We destroy the infrastructure and let the zombies loose."

"What about when they ask us where we got the Locker from?"

"Only Bart Romney and Dr. Riwazzo knows the answer. God rest their souls."

Charles hung up.

An article in a leading American newspaper soon after.

Was Locker extracted from zombies?

The drug, the infamous Locker, can no longer be used or manufactured in the country.

Matt, a resident of Stillwater Oklahoma has put forward an interesting theory. He claims that the drug is no longer manufactured because the raw material for the drug dried out. Zombies which were now dead and buried, figuratively and literally.

He claims that a virus, as cited in a research paper released in 2015, was developed to combat depression which is a common ailment affecting humans. It was this virus which had mutated into a demonic creature and eventually become a threat to mankind. This virus was referred to as the zombie bug at that time.

The virus had mutated in a rat while it was being experimented on the general populice. Matt claims that the anti-thesis of the virus, i.e. mutating the drugs to an opposite extreme, is what led to the discovery of the 'Locker' drug. And once the zombies were destroyed, the drug could no longer be manufactured.

The drug had attracted international criticism for our country as many distinguished people from across the world accused the drug of making people lazy and disinterested. This would have had major ramifications for the world economy, they claim.

Matt accused Ray Burburry, the President and owner of the pharmaceutical giant who manufactured and marketed the drug to the citizens of 'New America'. According to Matt, Burburry's research facility was underground and impenetrable. He also exploited the para-military team, The Security Detail and defeated the purpose with which this special body was formed. For the first time in American history, a shrewd man's greed has jeopardised the survival of the entire human race.

Click   http://www.oklahomadaily.com/menacethathaunted mankind.html=zombies=Burburry=threat to read more about where Matt spent the two years of his life and how he kept himself alive amidst the undead and lost a dear friend who ended up becoming a zombie himself.

Matt's story remains uncorroborated.